# BLACKBEARD'S REVENGE

LEGACY PRESS
www.LegacyPressKids.com

# BLACKBEARD'S REVENGE

## A TIME CRASHERS Adventure

### BY
H. MICHAEL BREWER

DEDICATION:
For Uncle Gil, half man and half fish!

TIME CRASHERS: BLACKBEARD'S REVENGE
© 2014 by Michael Brewer
ISBN 10: 1-58411-157-7
ISBN 13: 978-1-58411-157-3
Legacy reorder #LP48703
JUVENILE FICTION / Religious / Christian / General


Legacy Press
P.O. Box 261129
San Diego, CA 92196
**www.LegacyPressKids.com**

Cover and interior illustrator: Aburtov and Graphikslava

Unless otherwise noted, Scriptures are from the *Holy Bible: New International Version* (North American Edition), ©1973, 1978, 1984 by the International Bible Society. Used by permission of Zondervan Bible Publishers.

*Printed in the United States of America*

# TABLE OF CONTENTS

# BLACKBEARD'S REVENGE

## Introduction

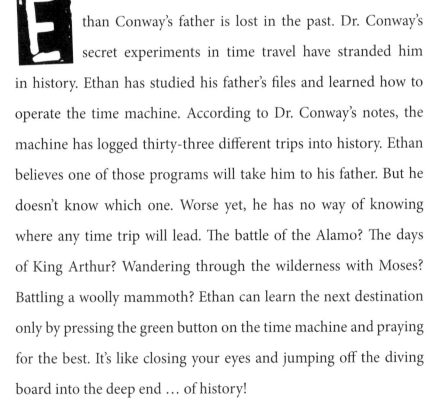

than Conway's father is lost in the past. Dr. Conway's secret experiments in time travel have stranded him in history. Ethan has studied his father's files and learned how to operate the time machine. According to Dr. Conway's notes, the machine has logged thirty-three different trips into history. Ethan believes one of those programs will take him to his father. But he doesn't know which one. Worse yet, he has no way of knowing where any time trip will lead. The battle of the Alamo? The days of King Arthur? Wandering through the wilderness with Moses? Battling a woolly mammoth? Ethan can learn the next destination only by pressing the green button on the time machine and praying for the best. It's like closing your eyes and jumping off the diving board into the deep end … of history!

Fortunately, Ethan isn't alone. Jake Bradley, an all-star athlete,

# TIME CRASHERS

and Spencer Price, a young genius, are like brothers to Ethan. Together they are the Time Crashers! And you are part of the team, too. You'll journey into the past with Ethan, Jake, and Spencer. You'll face the same risks, and you'll wrestle with tough decisions. Be careful! How this story turns out is up to you. Some paths lead to success and others to grim defeat and death.

## ADVENTURE IS WAITING. CLEAR YOUR MIND. PUMP UP YOUR COURAGE. TAKE A DEEP BREATH!

 WHEN YOU ARE READY TO LEAP INTO THE SWIRLING MISTS OF HISTORY, TURN THE PAGE. ⟶

## Yo-ho-ho! Away we go!

**M**iss Wigger stirs a pot of potato soup and smiles as Ethan, Jake, and Spencer troop through the kitchen on a Friday afternoon. "Heading for the basement?" she asks. "You boys spend so much time down there, you're going to turn into moles."

"The basement is our, uh, club house," Ethan stammers, glancing at his pals.

"For our History Club," Spencer explains. The compact boy nudges Jake. "We love the past, right?"

"Oh, yeah," the blond athlete nods enthusiastically. "You'd be surprised how exciting it is to learn about Vikings and volcanoes. You wouldn't believe the toilets in ancient Rome! Instead of toilet paper—"

"I'll stick with modern plumbing," Miss Wigger says, waving

her hand to cut off Jake's explanation. "Ethan, remember your book report is due on Monday."

"Don't worry," Ethan promises. "I'll work on it after, uh, our History Club meeting."

The boys descend the basement steps, locking the door behind them. As Ethan uses the palm print reader to open the hidden door into the sub-basement, Jake asks, "How long before your housekeeper gets suspicious?"

"I don't know," Ethan answers, sounding worried. "Miss Wigger is used to Dad taking off on government assignments for weeks at a time. But it's just a matter of time before she wonders why we haven't heard from him."

"But time is on our side," Spencer grins, his brown eyes twinkling eagerly. "We have a time machine."

The time travel device fills most of the sub-basement. It's a horseshoe shaped hulk of consoles, blinking lights, switches, and LED indicators.

The boys take their usual places on a metal disc set into the concrete floor.

"Quick review," Ethan says. "We have forty-eight hours in the past. That's max. Once each hour, the retrieval pulse will reach for us. If we're in the right place—the place we first appear—the pulse will bring us home. After two days, the time machine turns off the pulse and we're stuck in the past."

"Do not pass Go. Do not come home. Do not collect two hundred dollars," Spencer quips.

"Exactly," Ethan nods. "The translation app on the machine will teach us whatever language we need to speak, so we won't have trouble communicating."

"And we can't leave anything in the past or bring anything back with us," Jake finishes impatiently. "Come on, let's get the ball in play."

Making sure all three Time Crashers are on the metallic plate, Ethan presses a green button on the control panel.

"All aboard the History Express," Ethan calls over the rising hum of the machine. The power crystal flares into scarlet brilliance, recalling the deadly glow of lava spewing from Mt. Vesuvius on their last adventure.

Ethan's skin tingles, a feeling like ants marching on his arms and neck. A vibration trembles through his backbone and into his belly. His gut quivers and lurches as if two teams are waging a paintball battle in his stomach. The throbbing hum drums in his ears, and the basement lab disappears.

# TIME CRASHERS

The noise of the time machine suddenly dies, replaced by the roar of a storm and the crash of thunder. Water pummels Ethan. Wind pounds his shivering body. Under his shoes, the deck tilts and Ethan tumbles into a free-fall. He reaches wildly, blinded by rain. One hand snags a rope. Clutching desperately with both hands, he 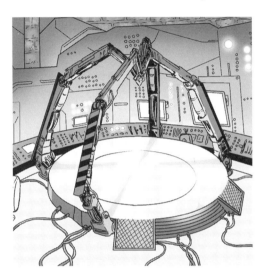 dangles in the air like a spider hanging by a single, fragile thread. Rain and wind batter him angrily.

*Gotta get down,* he thinks. *Get solid ground under my feet or I'm a goner.*

Hand over hand, he scrambles down the rough rope. Sometimes he locks his feet around the heavy cord, but they quickly entangle with other ropes. As the wind whips him back and forth, he bangs against rough timber, bruising his sides and back.

*Where is Jake?* he wonders. *And Spencer? Are they safe?*

A fierce gust forces his attention back to the risky descent. He wiggles free of a tangle of lines and continues down the rope. His last drop of strength is draining away when he feels wooden boards

beneath his feet. He settles on the rocking floor, resting his aching shoulders and arms, balancing on the balls of his feet.

"Thank you, God," he whispers. "Please, take care of my friends."

"Beware, boy!" a voice shouts over the screeching wind.

From the corner of his eye, Ethan glimpses movement. Something slams his temple, and darkness drags him into unconsciousness.

 TURN TO PAGE 14.

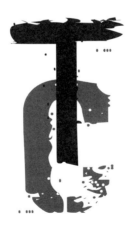

finger rolls back Ethan's eyelid and a light stabs his eye. A moment later, his other eye is forced open to the light. Rubbing his head tenderly, Ethan sits up in a small room illuminated by a few streaks of sunlight.

"His pupils look okay," Spencer says, returning a small flashlight to Jake, who tucks it into one of the many pockets in his vest.

"What hit me?" Ethan asks.

"A yardarm broke loose and smacked you royally," Jake says admiringly. "Like a hammer on a pumpkin. You've been out for hours."

The floor rolls gently and Ethan guesses, "We're on a ship?"

"Yeah," Jake says. "We popped in during an epic storm."

"We materialized on a lookout platform high on a mast," Spencer explains.

14

"The crow's nest," Ethan says. "Awesome."

"They won't call it a crow's nest for a few more decades," Spencer informs him, "but basically you're right. On these sailing ships the best way to look for land or bad weather is to send someone up on the mast for the long view."

"The wind yanked you off before we could grab you," Jake says, grinning. "Spence and I held onto that mast like Dr. Octopus, but you looked like Spider-Man climbing down that rope."

"I don't feel like a superhero; more like a sponge in the garbage disposal," Ethan admits. "What's the date?"

"Sometime in the early 1700s," Spencer says. "At least that's my guess. But our problem right now isn't the *when*; it's the *who*."

"I'm not in the mood for Twenty Questions," Ethan grumbles. He gingerly touches the bump on his temple. "If there's bad news, spit it out."

"I've overheard the crew talking about the ship's captain," Spencer says. "His name is Teach. Edward Teach. Does that ring any bells?"

Ethan shakes his head, and squints against the pain in his skull.

"Edward Teach is better known as—"

Banging timber and flooding sunlight interrupt Spencer as an overhead door flies open. A mocking voice calls down, "Come out, bilge rats. The captain wants to see you."

The Time Crashers climb a crude ladder onto the deck of the great ship. Three masts soar overhead, pointing into a cloudless sky. The ship is about one hundred feet long, and the height of the masts is as great as the length of the ship.

Ethan gulps. "I climbed down from there?"

"The tallest mast, the one in the middle," Spencer tells him.

"Aye, that you did," agrees the taunting voice, "with all the grace of a drunken, peg-legged monkey."

Ethan turns toward the mocking figure. The sailor is tall and slender, dressed in loose pants, a calico shirt, and a knee-length jacket of coarse brown cloth. A bright sash wraps the waist of the white pants, a knife tucked beneath the crimson cloth. Amused eyes measure Ethan from the shade of a three-cornered hat.

Ethan studies the sailor's delicate features and sandy hair. His eyes widen.

"You're a girl!" he gasps.

"Almost as smart as a monkey, too," she says. She indicates the ship with a sweep of her hand. "Welcome to *Queen Anne's Revenge*. You can call me Long Liz."

"*Queen Anne's Revenge?*" Spencer cries. "Oh, no. Why am

I almost always right?"

"You're not right this time, African," Long Liz corrects him. "You picked the wrong ship to hide on. You and your mates couldn't be more wrong."

She beckons for them to follow. Ragged crewmen mend ropes and patch sails, repairing storm damage. They eye the boys suspiciously. One man sits propped against a mast. His skin is milky pale, his expression twisted by pain. His left leg is wrapped in stained bandages. As the time travelers pass, Ethan wrinkles his nose at the odor of the man's wound.

Long Liz leads them to a slightly raised section of the deck at the rear of the ship, then down steps to a lower passage. She knocks on a door and a gruff voice calls, "Enter!"

"Maybe I'll see you later," Liz says, grinning crookedly. "But probably not."

She opens the door and pushes the boys inside, slamming it behind them. The room is surprisingly spacious, with a cabinet, a well-cushioned bunk, and a table strewn with maps and charts. A man sits at the table, his back to the door. He drains a pewter mug, wipes his mouth, and rises from the chair. He turns to face the boys.

He is well over six feet tall with broad shoulders and huge hands. Curly black hair falls to his shoulders. Hanging across his thick chest is a bushy beard, tied into separate strands with bright

red ribbons. Leather boots rise to mid-thigh. A white, frilly shirt peeks between the lapels of a long scarlet coat with tails and wide cuffs. He studies the boys with keen, shrewd eyes.

"I'm Blackbeard," the man says in a deep, rumbling voice, "and you are stowaways on my ship."

Ethan stares at the pirate captain in awe, barely able to believe that he is face to face with the legendary Blackbeard.

"What are you called?" Blackbeard asks.

The boys give their names and the huge man nods thoughtfully.

"Well, Ethan, Jake, and Spencer, can you give me one reason," asks the pirate, "why I shouldn't cut you up for fish bait?"

 IF YOU YOU THINK ETHAN SHOULD SPEAK UP, CONTINUE TO **PAGE 21**.

 IF YOU THINK JAKE SHOULD TRY TO CONVINCE BLACKBEARD NOT TO THROW THEM OVERBOARD, TURN TO **PAGE 25**.

We're here to sign the Articles," Ethan announces confidently. "A pirate crew can always use good men, and we've come to join."

"The Articles?" Jake whispers to Spencer.

Ethan shoots him a warning glare.

"The Articles," Ethan repeats. "The signed agreement that lays out the rules on this ship. No smoking or open lanterns in the gunpowder room. No stealing of food. An equal share of treasure for each man, except the captain, the quartermaster, and the first mate—who all get extra."

"So you know all about life on a pirate ship?" Blackbeard muses.

"I know things you don't know," Ethan says, taking a risk.

"Aye?" Blackbeard asks, his voice as low and threatening as a

rumble of thunder.

"That man up on the deck with the bandaged leg," Ethan says. "I can save him."

"His wound has gone foul," Blackbeard says. "Poor Samuel is dead and doesn't know it."

"No," Ethan insists. "The wound has gangrene—dead flesh—that needs to be cleaned out. I know how to do it."

The pirate strokes his beard and waits for Ethan to continue.

"Send someone to the food stores below and have them gather a cup of maggots," Ethan instructs. Blackbeard's eyebrows rise. Ethan explains, "The hatchings from fly eggs."

"I know what they are, boy," Blackbeard rasps. "Don't mistake me for a dullard."

"Put the maggots in Samuel's wound," Ethan continues. "They will eat the gangrene—the rotten skin—without harming the healthy flesh."

"You know this will work?" Blackbeard asks.

"I know it is that man's best chance," Ethan says confidently.

After a long moment of silence, Blackbeard nods. "I'll order the ship's surgeon to see to it. If Samuel lives, you and your mates have a place on this ship as long as you wish to stay."

"What if he dies?" Jake asks.

"We'll send his corpse to the bottom of the sea," Blackbeard promises, "and you'll keep him company."

 TURN TO **PAGE 36**.

# THE TEN ARTICLES

Many pirate ships had a written list of rules called the Articles of Agreement. God has given us our own Articles of Agreement called the Ten Commandments. You can read these ten rules in your Bible at Exodus 20:3-17 or you can replace the marked words below with the right rhyming words. Hood duck! Uh, I mean, good luck!

1. Don't *warship* any other gods.

2. Don't make any *snake rods.*

3. Don't *tissues* God's name.

4. Keep one *goalie ray* for God each week.

5. Honor your *bother and smother.*

6. Don't *chill* anyone.

7. Don't break your *carriage cows.*

8. Don't *squeal* somebody else's stuff.

9. Don't *sell fries* about people.

10. Don't sit around *fishing for rings* that belong to other people.

**SEE ANSWERS ON PAGE 200.**

**Y**ou need good men, and here we are," Jake says. "Yo-ho-ho and a bottle of rum."

The captain rakes dirty fingers through his oily beard. "How be you in a fight?" the pirate asks. "Can you handle yourselves when swords clash and cannon balls fly?"

Jake thumps a fist on his chest. "Bring it on," he boasts.

"Dial it down a few notches," Ethan whispers.

A wicked smile tugs at one corner of Blackbeard's mouth. "I have to know that your big talk is more than swagger."

He leads the boys back onto the deck. Curious pirates look up from their chores. Blackbeard seizes a bucket of food scraps, mostly bones and fish heads. He dumps the bucket over the rail, then pitches the empty bucket into the sea after the scraps.

"How clumsy of me," the captain mutters. "I need someone to fetch that bucket." He squints at Jake. "Someone brave and bold, someone who wants to prove himself."

"Fine," Jake says. "I'm in the mood for a swim. How do I get back on the ship?"

"We'll throw you a line," Blackbeard promises.

Jake strips off his vest and shirt, and kicks off his shoes. He climbs atop the rail and extends his hands for a dive.

"This is too easy," Ethan says to Spencer. "I don't like it."

"Let's hope those scraps don't attract—" Spencer breaks off his comment, scanning the water, shading his eyes against the sunlight reflecting from the waves. "Is that a fin?"

"Don't do it, Jake!" Ethan cries. "Shark!"

But Jake has already leaned into his dive. His arms pinwheel as he fights for balance, but he falls forward. At the last second, he pushes off with strong legs and cuts the blue water with a clean dive. His head bobs back to the surface, and Jake looks around in alarm. Ten yards away, the shark fin traces a circle around the swimmer.

Ethan grabs a coil of heavy rope and runs for the rail, but Blackbeard swings a huge fist and knocks him to the deck. When Spencer clutches the rope, the captain barks, "Hold 'em, lads!" Four pirates seize the struggling boys, one clutching each arm.

"Long Liz," Blackbeard calls to the female pirate. "Fetch my musketoon, if you please."

Jakes sees the fin turn in his direction. The bucket bobs at his shoulder. Maybe if he grabs the bucket, Blackbeard will throw him a line. Or should he keep his hands free to fight the shark?

 IF YOU YOU THINK JAKE SHOULD GRAB THE BUCKET, CONTINUE TO **PAGE 28**.

 IF YOU YOU THINK JAKE SHOULD IGNORE THE BUCKET, TURN TO **PAGE 31**.

The shark speeds toward Jake, his open mouth showing rows of vicious teeth. An instant before the shark strikes, Jake snags the bucket and shoves it into the gaping mouth. He pushes with both hands and the pail wedges into the killer's maw.

The shark shakes its head wildly from side to side. Thrashing angrily, the shark's powerful jaws crush the wooden bucket in a wet spray of shards and splinters.

Jake locks a piece of jagged wood in each fist. As the predator comes in for the kill, the time traveler maneuvers his knee toward the shark's mouth.

The shark bites Jake's leg, but the heavy fabric of his cargo pants and the supplies in his bulging pockets offer momentary protection from the cruel teeth. In that second, Jake stabs his wooden weapons

# TIME CRASHERS

at the beast's eyes. The hungry eyes are small and set back from the blunt nose. In the foaming water, Jake's not sure if he hits either eye or both, but the shark bucks in pain or sudden fury and releases its hold on the athlete's leg.

Swirls of blood paint the water, either from Jake's leg or from the injured shark—if the wooden shards have really done any damage.

Jake always brings weapons and supplies when time traveling. More than once a piece of twine or a flare or a balloon have saved the Time Crashers in a tight spot. Many of his emergency tools are in his vest on the deck of the *Queen Anne's Revenge*. Mind racing, Jake wonders if he has something that might even his odds in this deadly fight. He gropes through his pockets but finds nothing hard or sharp.

The fin approaches again, slicing through the water like a deadly blade. Jake doubts he can survive another attack, but he spits water from his mouth and shouts, "Come on, you slimy bottom-feeder! Let's finish this!"

 TURN TO **PAGE 33**.

 don't know if I can beat you," Jake yells at the shark, "but I'm not gonna play dead."

Jake is both a wrestler and a boxer. Hours pounding the heavy bag and the speed bag, pumping iron, and sparring with buddies in the community gym have taught him to throw a shattering punch. As the shark draws near, Jake kicks hard, raising his upper body from the water, and drives his fist down into the nose of the shark. The fish, confused by the attack, swerves away.

Jake wiggles his aching hand in the cool water. "I hope that hurt you as much as it hurt me," he says.

The fish circles and attacks again. Most swimmers never see a shark until it bites. Jake has an advantage because he can track the killer's movements. When the shark is within reach, Jake punches wildly at the snout above the open mouth, pounding with both hands. Again the deep-sea hunter darts aside, but the desperate athlete hooks one hand in the shark's gills. Jake yanks and claws at the tender gills, feeling the flesh tear. The shark half-rises from the water in pain, jerks loose from its enemy's grip, and thrashes the sea in fury. Streaks of blood swirl in the froth.

Tiny black eyes fix on Jake and the shark rockets toward the swimmer like a torpedo. Panting, knuckles bleeding, and too slow to escape, Jake waits for the hungry mouth to close on him.

"Choke on it," he shouts, fists raised in defiance.

 TURN TO **PAGE 33**.

A roar splits the air, like a small explosion on board the ship. The approaching shark arches in pain, blood spurting from a ragged wound on its head. Whether dying or merely injured, the shark gives up on Jake and dives beneath the waves, disappearing except for a spreading stain of blood on the surface of the water.

Jake looks up at the ship and sees Long Liz with one boot propped on the deck rail. In her arms is a rifle of some kind, smoke curling from the flared barrel. She smiles smugly and touches her hat brim with one finger in a mock salute.

A rope uncurls and falls toward Jake.

"Hold fast," calls a sandy-haired man with a short beard. "We'll hoist you aboard."

"I don't need your help," Jake shouts. "Just tie it off."

Although his arms are trembling with stress and fatigue, Jake climbs the rope hand over hand and hauls himself onto the deck.

"Where's my bucket?" Blackbeard growls. For a moment his expression is fierce, then he throws back his head and laughs lustily. As the pirate roars in humor, Jake pulls on his shirt, vest, and shoes. Wiping his eyes, the captain slaps Jake on the back, nearly knocking him to his knees. "You're a game lad! And your mates would have jumped in behind you if we hadn't held them back. I like loyalty; it proves a man's character."

"Does that mean we've earned a place in your crew?" Jake asks.

 TURN TO PAGE 38.

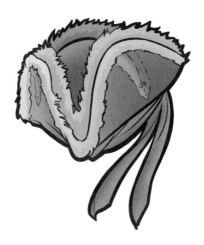

## WEIRD AND WACKY PIRATE FACTS

**PIRATES HAD MEDICAL INSURANCE.** If a pirate got hurt in a battle, he was paid for his injuries. On one ship, the loss of a finger or an eye was worth 100 gold coins. Losing the left arm brought 500 coins, and the right arm was worth 600. A broken fingernail was worth nothing.

**PIRATES WORE DRESSES—SOMETIMES.** In order to appear harmless as they approached another ship, pirate crews sometimes dressed as women. Imagine the surprise of the other ship when the "ladies" whipped out pistols and swords!

**PIRATES WORE EARRINGS INSTEAD OF GLASSES.** Many people in pirate days believed that piercing one's ear would improve eyesight. It doesn't work. And piercing an eyebrow won't improve your sense of smell, either.

**GOLD EARRINGS PAID FOR A FUNERAL.** If a pirate was lost at sea, he hoped that his body would wash ashore and someone would take his earring in trade for a decent burial. But would you want to pluck the earring from a waterlogged body?

**NO JONAHS ALLOWED!** If a ship was having lots of trouble, the crew might decide that someone on board was a Jonah, a bad luck magnet, and throw him overboard. What if the ship's luck doesn't improve after the Jonah is pitched? Darn, it must have been the wrong guy!

**B**lackbeard leads the boys on deck, and calls for the ship's doctor, a bow-legged man in a yellow shirt and filthy britches. Ethan oversees pouring the heap of squirming white maggots into the ragged wound on Samuel's leg.

"When the gangrene has been eaten away, remove the maggots and wash the wound twice a day in rum. Change the bandages after each washing," Ethan instructs the medic.

"A waste of good rum," the doctor complains, "but whatever the captain wants."

As the doctor wraps a clean bandage around the maggot-filled injury, Jake whispers, "Where did you learn that a maggot a day keeps the gangrene away?"

"It's a treatment they used in the Civil War," Ethan says. "I saw it on TV."

"Isn't it Spencer's job to come up with brilliant ideas like that?" Jake kids, glancing at his straight-A pal.

Spencer doesn't notice the jab. He seems distracted and worried.

"Are we in your crew?" Ethan asks Blackbeard.

 TURN TO PAGE 38.

**M**ayhap," the pirate captain answers. "We'll settle the question later. For now, there is work to do. My first mate has spotted a ship. The other ships in my fleet are out scouting, but luck is on our side. The next kill will be ours."

The first mate, a sandy-haired sailor named Israel Hands, nods vigorously. "Looks to be flying a French flag," Hands says. "Maybe a slaver."

Blackbeard nods in satisfaction. "Proceed, Mr. Hands."

Hands grins, showing a broken front tooth. "All hands hoay!" he shouts, calling the crew to readiness. Pirates leap into action hoisting sails, turning the huge capstan to raise the anchor, and loading the cannons. First Mate Hands personally hoists the ship's flag. Ethan eyes the fearsome image as it rises in the wind. On a black flag stands a horned skeleton holding an hourglass in one bony hand and a spear in the other.

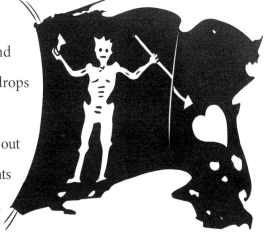

The point of the spear pierces a red heart and scatters three bright drops of blood.

"Time has run out for anyone who fights Blackbeard," Ethan says, watching the spooky banner flap. "That's what the hourglass means."

"How do you know so much about pirates?" Jake asks.

"I've always thought pirates were super cool," Ethan explains, "ever since I was a little kid. I used to run around the house in an eye patch waving a plastic cutlass. I've read every book on pirates in the school library."

 TURN TO PAGE 41.

## FLYING THE FLAG

Pirate captains designed flags that filled the heart with fear. Calico Jack Rackham's flag showed two crossed swords under a skull. Thomas Tew's flag depicted a muscular arm holding a cutlass, and Ned Lowe drew a skeleton on his banner.

How about a flag to make people feel good? What would that look like? What kind of flag would give people hope and joy? Try your hand at designing a flag like that. Draw in symbols that remind us that Jesus loves us and God watches over us.

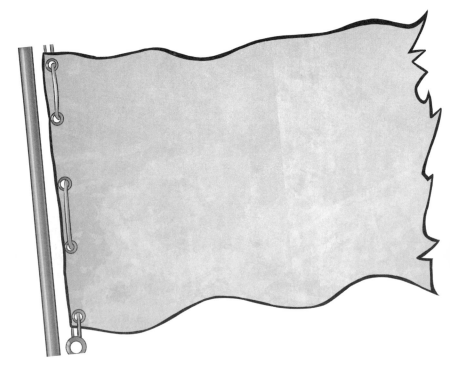

than, be careful with all that reading," Jake warns. "You'll turn into Spencer."

The young genius ignores the crack, his eyes squinting in thought.

"Hey, Einstein! Pay attention when I'm insulting you," Jake says.

"Hmmm?" Spencer asks. "Were you talking to me?"

Jake shakes his head and turns to Ethan. "What's the plan, boss man?"

"Ask around about my dad," Ethan says. "Show the drawing of his face to the sailors. Even if we don't find him aboard the *Queen Anne's Revenge,* we need to be sure he's not on one of Blackbeard's other ships."

Ethan looks at the swirl of activity on the ship as pirates angle sails in the wind and strap on swords. Already they draw nearer to the other ship. They are close enough for Ethan to read the name painted on the prow: *Le Lac Noir.*

"But our first job is to survive this battle," Ethan decides. He lowers his voice. "Be very careful of Blackbeard. He might seem friendly, but he's dangerous and unpredictable."

With a clatter, Israel Hands drops a small selection of swords on the deck at their feet.

"Cap'n says you'll be the first to board the enemy ship." Hands grins. "Either he likes you or he wants to be rid you."

The boys sift through the weapons and pick their blades.

"The first to charge onto the enemy ship," Ethan groans. "How do we get through this without getting killed and without killing somebody else?"

"Any ideas, Spencer?" Jake asks.

"It doesn't make any difference what we do," Spencer answers slowly.

"How do you figure that?" Jake asks impatiently.

"We're never going home," Spencer snaps. "Haven't you put the pieces together? We're stranded forever in Pirateville."

"Spit it out," Ethan says, a knot in his stomach.

"The retrieval pulse that takes us home," Spencer explains wearily, "is always tied to the place we first appear. On our trip to Lindisfarne it was a spot on the beach near a standing cross. In ancient Pompeii the pulse was locked to a location in an olive grove."

"So what?" Jake challenges.

But Ethan already sees what Spencer is saying. The knot in his gut yanks even tighter.

"How are we going to find our way back to a spot fifty feet in the air somewhere in the middle of the ocean?" Spencer asks.

Jake's mouth falls open and he turns to scan the horizon of endless ocean and sky.

"No landmarks," Jake mutters. "No signposts. Nothing to guide us to the removal bus."

"Now you're getting the picture," Spencer nods. "It's not like we have a helicopter and a GPS. First we have to find the exact location in thousands of miles of ocean—which we can't. Then we have to convince Blackbeard to take us back—which he won't. We need to find the pulse within the next forty hours—not a chance. Finally, we'd have to hold the ship in the exact spot while we wait for the pulse to activate—like balancing a Ping-Pong ball on the crest of a wave."

"In other words …" Ethan begins, but Spencer finishes the sentence.

"Bye-bye laptops, NASCAR, and french fries," Spencer laments. "Adios movies, motor scooters, and milkshakes. Sayonara families, homes, and the 21st century."

Ethan wonders if this explains his father's disappearance. What if Dr. Conway materialized in midair over the ocean with no ship below his feet? A plunge into the sea, a few hours treading water, and then … He shakes his head, trying not to picture his dad's death in the lonely waves.

 TURN TO **PAGE 47**.

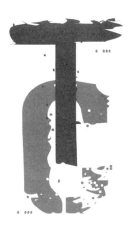

BURIED TREASURE

## DEAD END?

It looks like Ethan, Jake, and Spencer have smacked into a dead end with no way to return to their own time. But God has power to open a path through dead ends! In Old Testament times, God's people were escaping from Egyptian soldiers when they came to the Red Sea. What a dead end! Angry soldiers behind and water in front. But a surprise was waiting for God's frightened people.

To find out what happened next, decode these coded verses from the Bible. How do you read the code? Easy! Wherever you see a 1, change it into A. Change 2 into B, 3 into C, 26 into Z, and so on. Get it? (And if you want to read the whole story, look it up in your Bible in chapter 14 of Exodus.) Ready ... set ... decode!

1-12-12   20-8-1-20   14-9-7-8-20   20-8-5   12-15-18-4    4-18-15-22-5

20-8-5   19-5-1   2-1-3-11   23-9-20-8   1   19-20-18-15-14-7   5-1-19-20

23-9-14-4   1-14-4   20-21-18-14-5-4   9-20

9-14-20-15   4-18-25   12-1-14-4.   20-8-5   23-1-20-5-18-19   23-5-18-

5   4-9-22-9-4-5-4,   1-14-4   20-8-5   9-19-18-1-5-12-9-20-5-19   23-5-

14-20   20-8-18-15-21-7-8   20-8-5   19-5-1   15-14

4-18-25   7-18-15-21-14-4.

See answers on page 200.

 don't buy it," Jake says. "We're alive. We've got hope."

"Use your head," Spencer urges. "There's no way home."

"My heart says there is," Jake insists. He looks at his friends, eyes flashing. "Are we quitters or fighters?"

Long Liz strides up to join the boys. "From the way you're holding those swords, you won't be around for supper."

"I guess we're going to be fighters, after all," Spencer says with resignation.

Ethan shrugs and admits, "The closest I've ever been to a cutlass is riding around in my cousin's rusted Oldsmobile."

"Mr. Hands, ready the grapples," Blackbeard roars.

He has reappeared on deck dressed for battle. He carries a razor-edged cutlass in his left hand. Three pairs of pistols hang from his neck

tied to long ribbons. Each pistol fires only once and then must be reloaded, so the pirate has six quick shots ready. He wears a three-cornered hat with a long feather fluttering in the breeze. Jammed in his hair and hanging below the brim of his hat are slow-burning fuses. The fire and smoke make him look like a demon, a sight guaranteed to terrify enemies.

At Blackbeard's order, pirates grab long ropes tied to iron hooks. They hurl the metal grapples across the water and hook onto the approaching ship. Pulling fiercely on the ropes, the pirates drag the two ships side by side. On the deck of *Le Lac Noir,* the sailors watch with fearful eyes.

"Boys, do you want my help?" Long Liz asks. "Or do you want to die?"

IF YOU THINK THE BOYS SHOULD TRUST LONG LIZ FOR HELP, CONTINUE TO **PAGE 50**.

IF YOU YOU THINK THE TIME CRASHERS ARE BETTER OFF ON THEIR OWN, TURN TO **PAGE 55**.

W e'll take whatever help we can get," Ethan assures her.

Long Liz nods, drawing a curved cutlass with her right hand and gripping a knife in her left.

"Lead the way," she says, gesturing her blade at the other ship. "As soon as you hit their deck, stoop down. I'll take it from there."

"Let's do it!" Ethan says to his friends. He lightly punches Spencer in the shoulder. "Get your head in the game."

With a shout, Ethan leads the charge. The air thunders with explosions and reeks with fumes, both from firing guns and from grenades lobbed by the pirates. The grenades are hollow iron balls. Some are stuffed with tar-soaked rags to create billows of smoke. Others, filled with gunpowder, nails, and broken glass, explode violently when the slow fuse burns down. The time travelers jump

onto the deck of *Le Lac Noir,* almost hidden by choking clouds. Following the orders of Long Liz, they drop immediately to all fours. Wind brushes their backs as the swordswoman leaps over them.

Long Liz lands in a crouch and her blade dances in a deadly blur—stabbing, jabbing, thrusting, and hacking. The cutlass moves faster than Ethan's eye can follow. By the time the boys climb to their feet, the French sailors are falling back from the fiery pirate girl. She laughs and drives them before her flashing iron.

The battle is a confusion of shouts and grunts, clashing blades, banging flintlocks, eye-burning smoke, and a deck slippery with blood. Ethan's head whips back and forth trying to follow the action, but the battle feels like a whirlpool of chaos. Figures lurch back and forth through the choking fumes. In the haze, it isn't always clear whether a fighter is a pirate or a French defender.

The bewildered Ethan has no idea which ship is winning. He's not even sure which side he wants to win. When one side is pirates and the other is slave-traders, there aren't any good guys to cheer for. He decides to concentrate on staying alive. Survival is the only victory that makes sense in this storm of violence.

A French sailor rushes at Ethan and swings his cutlass in an overhead arc. Ethan raises his own blade just in time to block the falling sword. Metal clangs against metal. The impact numbs Ethan's fingers and he struggles to cling to his weapon. Something strikes

the Frenchman from behind. A musket ball? A piece of shrapnel from a grenade? The point of a dagger? Ethan's attacker cries out. He staggers across the wet deck and stumbles over the rail into the sea.

A stray grenade thuds to the deck near Jake, who kicks it toward the main mast just before it explodes. The blast riddles the smoky air with flying splinters and chunks of timber. Almost as quickly as the fight began, the violence suddenly subsides. The French sailors lay down their swords.

"Mercy!" they cry. "We beg for quarter!"

 TURN TO PAGE 61.

**T**hanks," says Ethan. "We've got our own plans."

Long Liz shrugs skeptically and strides away, one hand resting on her sword.

"We've got a plan?" Jake asks.

Muskets and flintlock pistols pop as the pirates pick off crew members on *Le Lac Noir*. Acrid gun smoke irritates the boys' lungs. Adding to the noise and confusion, a laughing pirate hurls a grenade onto the approaching ship. The iron ball rolls across the French deck, fuse sputtering, and explodes in a deadly spray of metal shards.

"The air is going to be thick with smoke," Ethan explains to Jake. "We can pull a few future tricks without getting caught. Can I borrow your pepper spray?"

From past adventures, Ethan knows that one of the items in

the athlete's utility vest is the eye-burning spray. A blast of the pepper concoction will drop a strong man without doing any real harm. Jake digs the small can from a pocket in his vest and pitches it to Ethan.

"You take point and I'll watch your back," Jake promises. A scurrying pirate accidentally drops a leather bag with a thud as he sprints past. The athlete grins and scoops it up. "If this is what I think, it might come in handy."

"Spencer!" Ethan shouts. The honor roll student turns a distracted gaze toward his buddies. "Focus! Stay behind us and don't get killed!"

The boys perch on the deck rail as the ships grind together, joined by the grapples. The pirates jump abroad the French ship.

"God, we're going to be too busy to pray," Ethan whispers, "but I know you won't be too busy to protect us."

Ethan leaps onto *Le Lac Noir*, and his buddies follow. Their feet have scarcely settled on the deck before a French sailor levels a pistol at Ethan. The time traveler sprays pepper juice into his face, and Jake's sword knocks the pistol aside as it goes off. A lead ball explodes into the mast. The sailor drops his gun and rubs frantically at his eyes, falling to the planks. As the pungent stench of peppers mingles with

the swirling clouds of smoke, Jake grabs the dropped flintlock and shoves it in his belt.

From that moment the battle turns into a chaos of charging bodies and clashing blades wrapped in blinding smoke. Ethan drops one sailor after another with the pepper spray. A huge sailor looms from the smoke, carrying a sword in one hand and a wicked hook in the other. Ethan presses the button, but the can fizzles, finally emptied.

"I got this one," Jake shouts and pulls the pistol from his belt. He aims the barrel with a steady hand. The flintlock has already been fired, but the charging Frenchman doesn't know the gun is empty. He raises arms over his face and dives into the smoke, disappearing from view.

Three more fighters charge the boys, sabers lifted.

"Stand your ground," Jake barks. He produces the pouch he picked up earlier and empties the contents. A cascade of lead musket balls scatters across the deck, rolling toward the running enemies. Two of the French sailors lose their footing like cartoon characters on banana peels. As they fall, one of their clutching hands drags down the third swordsman.

The deck, slippery with blood, is littered with moaning men and lost weapons. The boys edge to a clear space, and Ethan shouts, "Back to back!" The Time Crashers cluster themselves and lift their swords for a last stand.

But as suddenly as the ferocious battle began, now it trails off. The Frenchmen, clearly defeated, lay down their arms.

"We surrender," a voice cries. "Why should we die for someone else's cargo?"

"White flag!" shouts another. "No more killing!"

TURN TO **PAGE 61**.

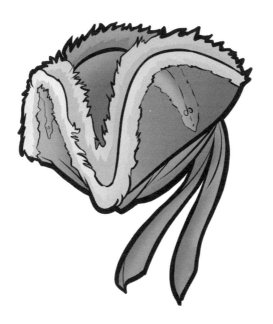

# OUR PROTECTOR

Either the Time Crashers just got really lucky or God kept them safe in the battle. Which do you think really happened?

David was a warrior in Bible times who fought many dangerous battles. Would you like to know what David says about God's protection? You can read David's message on the word wheel below. Start with the letter on top of the wheel—the large T—and copy down every second letter. Be sure you move clockwise—that is from left to right. When you've been around the word wheel twice, you'll have the whole message.

See answer on page 200.

B lackbeard strides across the captured deck, blood dripping from his sword and smoke curling from the barrels of the flintlock pistols hung around his neck. With a mighty hand, he hoists a wounded French sailor to his feet.

"Where is your captain?" the pirate asks.

The bleeding sailor points to a man leaning against a mast. The French captain's angry face is streaked with smoke stains and blood. His hat is missing, and the powdered wig popular among the well-to-do tilts sideways on his head. His right hand still clutches a sword, but the arm dangles at his side, apparently lifeless. Blackbeard stomps across the wet planks and confronts the French commander. With a flick of his own blade, the pirate flips the Frenchman's sword free and sends it clattering across the deck.

The French leader offers a left-handed salute and says, "Capitaine Ricou Marron at your service, Monsieur Blackbeard."

"I don't need your service," Blackbeard snarls, "just your cargo."

"We are carrying African slaves bound for the auction block in Charleston," Marron says.

"I wouldn't want to be wearing your boots, Frenchie," Blackbeard says, shaking his head in mock pity. "A lot of my crew are former slaves, and they don't like people who buy and sell human lives." Blackbeard raises his voice. "It's a slave ship, lads! Free the poor souls in the hold, and deal with the captain as you wish."

A circle of pirates gather around Marron. Most of them are black; probably once they were slaves themselves.

One pirate, his head wrapped in a red bandana, says, "Let's see him dance the hempen jig."

"After we keelhaul him," says another.

 CONTINUE TO **PAGE 63**.

**E**than looks on in horror. He hates the idea of selling God's children as slaves, but Ricou Marron is also one of God's children—even if he has done terrible things. Human life is precious in God's eyes. Given a second chance, maybe Marron can become a better person.

Ethan seizes a piece of broken timber as large as a fireplace log. He pushes through the ring of pirates. He screams, "Slave-selling scum! Bilge rat!"

Ethan rams the surprised captain with the piece of wood. The Frenchman staggers backward and his wig falls off. The pirates laugh and open a way for him through the circle. Ethan pushes the timber against his chest again, and once more Marron stumbles back.

With a final lunge, Ethan hurls the broken wood at the slave trader.

The timber thumps into his chest. He catches it awkwardly with his left arm, but the weight forces him backwards over the rail of the deck and into the sea. The pirates applaud Ethan with whistles and cheers. One squinting crewman slaps Ethan on the back. "Well done, mate," he says. "Let the scurvy dog sleep with Davey Jones tonight."

The pirates drift off to other duties, freeing slaves from the ship's hold, plundering goods from the French captain's cabin, and shifting food and supplies to the *Queen Anne's Revenge*. Jake leans near to Ethan, his eyes wide and expression disbelieving.

"You just pushed Captain Marron overboard!" he whispers urgently. "Are you crazy?"

"I saved his life," Ethan replies in a low voice. "At least I hope so. There's land on the horizon and no sharks in sight. If he hangs onto that timber, he should be able to kick his way to shore."

"What if he's too weak?" Jake asks.

"At least he's got a chance," Ethan argues. "Do you know what the pirates were planning for him? The 'hemp jig' is slang for hanging a man. Keelhauling is worse. It means dragging a man underwater from the rear of the boat to the front, from stern to stem. If the victim survives drowning, the rough barnacles that grow on the bottom of the boat shred his skin until he looks like a hunk of raw meat. If he's lucky, the blood will draw the sharks to finish him quickly."

Jake's tan face turns almost milky white.

"These are not nice people," he mutters.

"No joke!" Ethan agrees. "Pirates seemed bold and exciting on paper. In real life, it's ugly."

 TURN TO **PAGE 68**.

## PIRATES AND PALS

Violence and stealing sometimes look good in movies, but never in real life. Would you want to chill with a buddy who steals from you? The Bible teaches us that "the righteous choose their friends carefully," because "bad company corrupts good character." (Proverbs 12:26; 1 Corinthians 15:33)

Here is a list of good qualities. Underline the ones that are important to you in finding friends. Circle the ones that are true about you.

BRAVE          GENTLE

HONEST

FUNNY

HELPFUL

TRUSTWORTHY          SMART

PATIENT

GENEROUS

KIND          FORGIVING

FRIENDLY     FUN

FAIR     RELIABLE

MODEST     TRUTHFUL

UNDERSTANDING

**S**o you made it," Long Liz observes as she strides past the boys.

"You don't have to sound so disappointed," Ethan snaps.

She shrugs. "If you caught a blade in the belly, I was going to claim your hat."

Ethan touches the bill of his baseball cap.

"This?" he asks in surprise.

"Very dashing. Maybe I'll grab it off your corpse after the next fight," she calls over her shoulder. "I wouldn't begin any long books if I were you."

The boys help load barrels and boxes onto the pirate ship, mostly food and ale. From Marron's cabin come sets of charts, a cask of medical supplies, bottles of French wine, and a few bolts of rich fabric. A drunken pirate drops a barrel which spills dried fish across the deck. From the corner of his eye, Ethan spies Spencer wrap one of the fish in a tar-stained rag and hide it in his pocket. *Midnight snack?* Ethan wonders.

By now the slaves have been brought to the deck. Some are dead from the terrible conditions in the hold of the ship where they were piled like human lumber. The bodies are thrown overboard, to join the dead sailors from *Le Lac Noir*. Although several pirates were wounded in the attack, none are dead.

The surviving Africans are half-starved, blinking in the bright sunlight. Some huddle fearfully; others are defiant.

"Who speaks English?" Blackbeard asks the crowd.

A tall African moves to the front. His ribs are visible beneath his dark skin, but his shoulders and arms are muscled, his stance proud.

"My name is Kwame. Your language is bitter on my tongue," he says, "but I speak it."

"Congratulations, Captain Kwame," says Blackbeard. "You are now the commander of *Le Lac Noir*."

"What do you mean?" asks the African, eyeing the pirate suspiciously.

"There are many sins on my conscience," Blackbeard answers, "but I am no slave trader. This ship is yours to sail where you will. Whatever French sailors still breathe will be your crew. You will

have swords and they will not, so I think they'll be happy to take you where you wish."

"I have a mind to see Jamaica," the black man says.

"Well said," Blackbeard agrees. "A beautiful island thick with thieves and running with rum. If any of my men wish to join you, will there be room?"

The new captain nods and turns away, speaking in an African tongue to some of the former captives. A ragged cheer rises among them. Kwame orders the dejected French sailors to prepare the ship for sailing.

Blackbeard climbs on the deck rail and gestures for Ethan to follow him back to *Queen Anne's Revenge*. The three time travelers return to the pirate ship and a huge heap of captured weapons.

"First to board gets first choice, a reward for bravery," Blackbeard announces and the pirates murmur in agreement. He pushes Ethan toward the pile. The time traveler's gaze sorts through the blades and firearms. He spots a gleaming sword with a razor edge, much nicer than the blade he received earlier from Israel Hands. The handle is protected by a basket hilt engraved with gold designs. He draws it from the tangle of weapons.

"I guess I'll take this one," Ethan says.

His choice is met with mutters of approval, except for one shirtless pirate with gold hoops in both ears and teeth nearly as yellow as the

earrings. A tattooed snake coils on his shoulder, the head just below his ear. Ethan wonders what the snake is whispering to the surly sailor.

"You've no right to that sword," says the tattooed man, his voice rough and rusty.

A chorus of voices cheers the challenger. "You tell him, Chappy Benjamin! Don't let the swabber steal your sword!"

Chappy's close-set eyes and flat nose remind Ethan of a reptile. He almost expects to see a forked tongue dart between the yellow teeth. The pirate mops his hairless head with a bandana. He curses foully. "I killed the man who carried that sword. It should be mine!"

Chappy drags a bloody rag across his sweaty face and swaggers to confront Ethan. "Hand it over," he orders, a sneer framing his stained teeth.

IF YOU THINK ETHAN SHOULD KEEP THE SWORD, TURN TO **PAGE 95**.

IF YOU THINK ETHAN SHOULD GIVE UP THE SWORD, CONTINUE TO **PAGE 74**.

"Give it up, hornswoggler," Chappy Benjamin growls, spitting on the deck at Ethan's feet.

Ethan shrugs. "Fair enough," he admits. "I didn't do anything to earn this sword. It should belong to someone who deserves it."

He studies the beautiful weapon, the sun glinting on gold and silver inlay. Carefully clutching the sharp blade, Ethan holds the handle out before him as if offering a gift. He moves toward the grinning Chappy Benjamin, passes by the stunned pirate, and gives the captured sword to Long Liz.

"This should be yours," Ethan says.

Liz accepts the sword, and tests the balance in her grip.

"You're right," Liz agrees. "This sword was made for me." She swings her gaze to Chappy. "If any man thinks differently, let him take it from me."

Chappy's beady eyes dart away from Liz's stare. He shoulders past Ethan, muttering, "We'll finish this later, boy."

"You're wrong, Chappy. We're finished now," Ethan calls after the sulking sailor. Turning to his friends, he adds, "And we're finished with this ship. We're leaving with the slaves."

"Good call," Spencer nods. "We're stuck in this century and we might as well make the best of it. Pirates live short lives."

"What makes you think the slave ship will be safer than the *Queen Anne's Revenge*?" Jake asks.

"I don't know what's waiting for *Le Lac Noir*," Ethan admits, "but I know how things turn out for Blackbeard. Trust me, we don't want any part of Blackbeard's last battle."

"If we stick with Blackbeard, we're sailing into disaster," Spencer says. "If we join the escaped slaves, we have at least a chance. How is this a hard choice?"

"Count me in," Jake says.

When Ethan tells Blackbeard of their decision, the big man nods agreeably. "Probably for the best," his deep voice rumbles. "Sail with me you'll likely come to a bad end."

"Doesn't that scare you?" Ethan asks.

"Everybody dies," Blackbeard says with a shrug. "If you die well, people will remember you. I plan to be remembered."

The pirate grabs Ethan's hand and shakes it.

"Good luck to you, lad, and fair weather," the pirate booms.

For a moment Ethan is thrilled to have shaken hands with a legend, but he feels something sticky. He discovers smears of blood on his fingers. Queasy, he wipes his hand on his jeans and returns to his friends. *Pirates are definitely better in library books,* he thinks. *Books never leave blood on your hands.*

The boys board *Le Lac Noir* and the former slave ship hoists sails into the wind. The *Queen Anne's Revenge* does the same, and the ships move away from each other. Soon the pirate ship is a tiny dot on the horizon. The freed slave Kwame struts up and down the deck, ordering and threatening the captured French crew.

"Kwame doesn't know anything about sailing. We're heading for trouble," Spencer says to his pals. "Shall I try to help him or should we take over the ship?"

# TIME CRASHERS

 IF YOU THINK SPENCER SHOULD OFFER ADVICE TO KWAME, CONTINUE TO **PAGE 78**.

 IF YOU THINK THE TIME TRAVELERS SHOULD TAKE CONTROL OF THE SHIP, TURN TO **PAGE 82**.

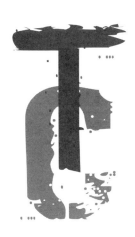

here's been enough fighting," Ethan suggests. "Maybe he'll listen to your advice."

With his friends at his side, Spencer approaches the African captain.

"Captain Kwame," Spencer says. "We should not sail so close to the shore. Hidden rocks can damage the ship."

"Fool!" Kwame says scornfully. "Would you take us into open sea and have us lose our way in the great ocean? As long as we keep the shore in sight, we cannot get lost."

"We can find our way using the stars," Spencer tells him. "I can teach you to navigate far from the land."

"You will teach me?" Kwame shouts. "You forget who is captain, but I will remind you."

The broad-shouldered African barks orders to the French crewman.

"Take us closer to shore," he commands.

The captured French sailors stare at one another in disbelief.

"The rocks," warns a Frenchman.

"You can face the rocks," Kwame screams, "or my blade!"

White-faced and shaken, the frightened sailors steer *Le Lac Noir* closer to the shoreline. "Please," one of them begs, "take us into open water."

Kwame seizes the shirt front of the pleading man and slaps him hard across the face.

"Do not fear the rocks," Kwame tells him, landing another slap. "Fear your captain!"

The angry African raises his hand again, but the ship lurches violently and the terrifying sound of breaking timbers splits the air. The deck tilts. A mast cracks and crashes across the bow. Kwame, his eyes mad with horror, loses his footing and falls over the railing into the sea. A French sailor tumbles after him.

A deep groan rumbles in the belly of *Le Lac Noir*. Caught on a hidden rock just beneath the surface of the sea, the ship is filling with water. As the tortured timbers twist, the craft breaks in two. Above the noise of shattering wood, screams ring out from both Africans and Frenchmen. Their differences are suddenly forgotten, washed away in the cold sea.

The Time Crashers cling together for a moment, but the violent

shattering of *Le Lac Noir* scatters them in the rolling waves. The remains of the ship sink rapidly, creating an undertow that drags all the swimmers down. In moments, the great ship is gone along with all its crew. Nothing remains to mark the passing of the slave ship except a few pieces of broken timber rolling on the waves and a bobbing red baseball cap.

# THE END

## YOU DON'T LIKE THIS ENDING?
## DO YOU WISH THE TIME CRASHERS HAD MADE OTHER CHOICES? GOOD NEWS! YOU HAVE A TIME MACHINE. GO BACK AND DO IT DIFFERENTLY.

THE FINAL ENDING IS UP TO YOU.

ake shakes his head sadly. "He's got the power and he's loving it. No way he's going to listen to anybody else."

Spencer climbs atop a barrel and shouts to the French soldiers and the milling Africans. Thanks to the time machine's language app, he moves easily from one language to another, speaking French for a moment, then repeating himself in several African languages.

"Do you want to die?" Spencer calls. "Do you want to sink into the sea and become food for the great monsters who live where the sun does not reach? If this is what you want, follow Captain Kwame and he will lead you to death. He sails too close to the shore. Rocks will find us and snap our ship like a twig."

Kwame glares at Spencer with bulging eyes. "Silence!" he shouts.

"Captain Kwame may be a brave man," Spencer says. "Maybe he is a wise man. But he does not know the sea. He cannot lead this ship."

"Lies!" Kwame roars. "I am captain. Who says I am not?" He waves his sword, slicing angry arcs in the air.

The French soldiers have no weapons. Some of the freed slaves carry swords, but they have spent weeks piled in the dark hold of the ship. Most of them are afraid. Their spirits are broken. Many of them have already watched loved ones die from hunger and disease. They have no heart for fighting, not even against a bully like Kwame.

"Time for Plan B," Spencer calls to his friends. "How about we dazzle them with wonders from the future, Jake? Flares. Laser pointers. Balloons. Whatever you can reach in a hurry."

But it's too late. Driven by Kwame's threatening sword, a dozen Africans rush the boys and drag them to the deck. In moments, they are tied and helpless.

"These strangers are dangerous," Kwame declares to the freed slaves, "but I am a man of mercy and peace. We will not kill them."

With his sword, he points to an island a few miles from shore.

"We will maroon them, leaving them on that island."

When they get close enough, the boys are rowed to the island in a dinghy—a small boat carried aboard the ship for short trips to land. Three frightened Africans push them from the dinghy into waist-deep water and row back toward *Le Lac Noir*. The Time Crashers wade ashore and help one another struggle free from their ropes.

"This is gonna be cool," Jake says, rubbing his chafed wrists. "I saw this TV show where they made all kinds of great stuff out of coconuts and palm leaves."

"Take a look around, Gilligan," Spencer sighs. "Not a tree in sight. Nothing but rocks, sand, and beach grass."

"So we'll fish," Jake suggests.

"Even if we could catch enough fish to feed all three of us, what are we going to drink?" Spencer asks. "This hunk of rock is drier than a bag of chalk dust."

"You want to give up and die?" Jake challenges.

"Give up or don't give up," Spencer says. "We die either way."

Ethan realizes he must bring his friends

together in a survival plan. He wonders if they are better off exploring the island or staying on the beach in hopes of spotting a ship.

 IF YOU THINK THE BOYS SHOULD EXPLORE THE ISLAND, CONTINUE TO **PAGE 87**.

 IF YOU THINK THE BOYS SHOULD WATCH FOR A SHIP, TURN TO **PAGE 89**.

et's explore," Ethan suggests. "Maybe the place isn't as barren as it seems."

With a sigh, Spencer rises to join the hunt.

The island turns out to be larger and richer than they imagined. At first, they survive on raw sea oats that grow along the shoreline. They forage shellfish from the beach, while they learn to weave oat-grass baskets that lure fish at high tide and trap them as the water recedes. They also gather eggs from sea birds nesting on the island.

Drinkable water is a problem, but near the center of the island is a rocky depression that collects rain. Since rain showers are frequent, the boys have just enough water to meet their needs. Over time, they arrange empty shells to gather additional rain.

As years pass, they find their simple existence comfortable and fulfilling. Now and again, they spot a ship in the distance, but the time travelers never try to hail passing vessels.

If they made their way back to "civilization" they would only be strangers in a world where they don't belong. Besides, their brief time with the pirates left them hungry for peace and harmony in a violent age.

They live long, satisfying lives, treasuring their friendship and sharing their faith. As time passes, Spencer is the last time traveler left alive. He spends his final months alone with his thoughts and his prayers. Using a stick to write in the sand, he works long, complicated mathematical problems.

He is not lonely. He has forgotten how to be lonely.

## THE END

YOU DON'T LIKE THIS ENDING?
DO YOU WISH THE TIME CRASHERS HAD MADE OTHER
CHOICES? GOOD NEWS! YOU HAVE A TIME MACHINE.
GO BACK AND DO IT DIFFERENTLY.

THE FINAL ENDING IS UP TO YOU.

than ignores the bickering. He shades his eyes and stares out to sea. *Le Lac Noir* has disappeared into the north, but a tiny white spot is visible in the south.

"Gather up all the dry grass and driftwood you can carry," Ethan orders, "and pile it on that hill. There's a ship coming this way."

Bounding through the hot sand and scrambling over bare rocks, the boys build a pile of brush and driftwood higher than their heads. By the time they finish, the sun is sinking into the sea. The white spot is still distant, but it has taken the shape of a ship under full sail. They sit beside the pile as full darkness falls. Deck lanterns help them track the progress of the ship.

"Okay, they're close enough," Ethan says. "Jake, do it."

The athlete pulls a road flare from his cargo pants and scrapes the tip across a rough stone. The flare erupts into a blinding torch, and Jake shoves it into the pile of dry grass and driftwood. In moments the bonfire is roaring, huge tongues of fire licking the sky.

"Jesus, you are the light of the world," Ethan prays. "We could use some extra light right now and a wide-awake sailor on that ship."

"Amen," Jake agrees.

"Ditto," Spencer adds.

They move away from the crackling heat, but the light of the flames makes it hard to see the ship.

"Has it stopped?" Ethan asks.

"I think so," Spencer says. "Or it's turned and is coming toward us."

They stay awake all night, and with the dawn they can see that the ship has anchored and a dinghy is rowing toward the island.

 CONTINUE TO **PAGE 91**.

**T**wo muscular sailors work the oars. When they are close enough, the three friends splash through the waves and clamber into the boat.

"Boy, are we glad to see you," Ethan says to the sailors.

"The British Royal Navy at your service," grins one of the sailors.

The other adds, "The captain of the man o' war *Samson* respectfully requests your presence for dinner."

"Just a tip, lads," the first sailor says. "The cap'n will be wanting to know who marooned you on that rock and why. If I were you, I'd make sure to have a good answer ready."

But no answer will be good enough to keep the Time Crashers out of trouble. As they climb the rope ladder to board the *Samson,* the first face they spot is the angry scowl of Capitaine Ricou Marron—the commander of the slave ship captured by Blackbeard.

"These three served on the pirate ship that attacked my vessel," Marron says. Pointing a trembling finger at Ethan, he adds, "And that killer threw me overboard. If you had not found me floating upon that piece of timber, I would surely have died in the sea."

A man in British uniform nods curtly to the boys. "I am Captain Harvey, Commander of His Majesty's Ship the *Samson*. In the name of King George, I arrest you for piracy on the high seas."

"We didn't choose to sail with Blackbeard," Ethan tells the red-faced Marron. "If I hadn't gotten you off the ship—"

The English captain cuts off the conversation with wave of his hand.

"Save your story for the jury," he orders. "English justice is fair to the innocent. If you were forced to sail with Edward Teach, if your motives toward Captain Marron were noble, you have nothing to fear. But if you are guilty of piracy, your days will be short and your end terrible."

The boys are confined below deck on rations of bread and water. As they mark the passing time in the cramped, dark room, they wonder what lies ahead. English courts in the American colonies are stern with pirates. But Ethan has read stories of people who were captured and forced to sail with pirates. Such victims are sometimes found innocent and set free by sympathetic juries.

"Remember how I prayed for help when we lit the bonfire?" Ethan reminds his friends. "That prayer turned out pretty well. We're off the island and on a ship."

"So maybe we should do more praying," Jake suggests.

Ethan nods.

"Let's pray that this ship is carrying us toward freedom," Ethan says. "Let's pray that the jury will find us innocent. Whatever is waiting for us in this century, let's pray for strength, wisdom, and courage."

"I want to live long enough to meet George Washington," Spencer says, his voice excited. "He'll be born in another ten or fifteen years."

"That sounds like the real Spencer," Jake says. "Have you decided to stop worrying?"

"Why worry? We may be lost in time," Spencer says, "but we're never lost from God."

## THE END

### YOU DON'T LIKE THIS ENDING?
### DO YOU WISH THE TIME CRASHERS HAD MADE OTHER CHOICES? GOOD NEWS! YOU HAVE A TIME MACHINE.
### GO BACK AND DO IT DIFFERENTLY.

THE FINAL ENDING IS UP TO YOU.

than doesn't care about the sword, but he dislikes bullies. If he gives in, every pirate on the ship will mark him as a cowardly weakling.

"Give it up, hornswoggler," Chappy Benjamin growls.

"If you want a prize sword," Ethan says, "next time have the guts to lead the boarding party instead of hiding in the pack."

His damp face reddening, Chappy draws his cutlass and crouches in a fighting stance. Before he can swing the blade, Blackbeard leaps between the two.

"You know the Articles," the captain tells the angry pirate. "No fighting on board the ship. Settle your quarrels on land."

"But this landlubber called me a coward!" Chappy shouts. "Pirate Code or not, I'm giving him a taste of cold iron."

Blackbeard's face darkens. With his own sword, he slices a five-foot piece of rope from a coil on the deck. He flings the rope at Chappy's feet. "The only tasting here will be the cat licking your blood, Mr. Chappy."

Ethan understands what the rope means. Chappy is about to be punished for disobeying orders. The pirate will have to unravel half the length of rope into nine strands and tie a knot in the end of each cord. Chappy's hands tied to a mast, another sailor will whip his bare back with the "cat o' nine tails."

"Defy the sea, if you like, Mr. Chappy," Blackbeard says coldly. "Defy the wind, if you dare. But never defy your captain."

"Aye-aye, Cap'n," Chappy nods, drops of sweat falling from his chin. As he begins to separate the strands of rope, he aims a murderous glare at Ethan. "Soon enough, we'll see if you know how to use that sword," he promises.

Blackbeard's angry mood passes as quickly as a cloud blowing past the sun. "Well done, my hearties," he calls to the crew. "Grab your black jacks! Bumboo all around!"

Shouts of joy ring across the ship, and pirates lift leather cups. The cups, called black jacks, have been dipped in tar to stiffen them and seal leaks. The ship's cook wrestles a barrel on deck and dips strong-smelling drink into the cups.

"Bumboo?" Jake asks.

"Rum, water, sugar, and nutmeg," Ethan says. "A real pirate treat."

Jake grimaces and shakes his head. "Do they know about plain water?"

"After a few weeks at sea, the drinking water is green and nasty," Ethan explains. "They mix it with rum to kill germs and cover the taste."

"I'm not thirsty after all," Jake decides.

From behind the boys, whacking sounds are accompanied by painful grunts. None of them turns toward the ugly noises, not wanting to see Chappy beaten with the cat o' nine tails.

Two galley hands carry a steaming kettle on deck, and the hungry crew gathers. One of the galley helpers pitches bowls and wooden spoons to the time travelers. "Grab some salmagundi," he suggests.

"I don't think my translation app is working," Jake whispers.

This time Spencer explains. "Stew made from chopped meat."

A scoop of the thick stew is plopped into Jake's bowl. "What kind of meat?" he asks, sniffing the aroma suspiciously.

"Whatever is handy," Spencer says. "Fish, salted pork, turtle."

"And cooked with cabbage, olives, grapes, anchovies, and cackle fruit," Ethan adds.

Despite his dark mood, Spencer grins. "Cackle fruit is pirate lingo for chicken eggs. They probably have hens on board."

Jake takes a tiny sip, then follows it with a brimming spoonful.

"Awesome!" the athlete says, licking his lips. "Ethan, you gotta get this recipe for Miss Wigger."

Spencer's momentary smile disappears, and his eyes grow gloomy. "We're not going home, remember?" he chides Jake. "We'll be dead five hundred years before Miss Wigger is born."

"Says you," Jake replies, speaking through a full mouth.

Before Spencer can argue, their attention is caught by the voice of Long Liz.

"Permission to go ashore, Cap'n," she says to Blackbeard. "We could use fresh fruit and clean water."

"Good thinking, lass. Mr. Hands, set a course into the sound, and load the cockboat with an empty barrel." Blackbeard turns toward the time travelers and asks, "Fancy a trip ashore, lads?"

"I don't need any help," Liz objects, glaring at Ethan.

IF YOU THINK THE BOYS SHOULD GO WITH LIZ, CONTINUE TO **PAGE 100.**

IF YOU THINK THE BOYS SHOULD STAY ON BOARD THE QUEEN ANNE'S REVENGE, TURN TO **PAGE 106.**

We'll go with Liz," Ethan says. "My feet want to walk on something that isn't moving."

"I'd rather go alone," Liz insists.

Ignoring her protest, Blackbeard adds, "Take Chappy, too. Might as well settle this quarrel before we head for open sea."

"Wonderful," Liz sighs. "I'll babysit while Chappy Benjamin and the swabber chop each other to fish bait."

"My name's not *swabber*; it's Ethan," the time traveler corrects her.

Long Liz stalks away and props one boot on the rail as the sails are shifted and *Queen Anne's Revenge* swings toward a finger of land. By the time the ship sails into the bay beside the peninsula, the young woman's temper has cooled. The ship's anchor is dropped into the sea, and Liz climbs into the cockboat, also called a dinghy, the small boat that carries crewmen back and forth to land.

"*Ethan*," she says, stressing his name with exaggerated courtesy, "please take a seat in the prow." Ethan squeezes around the empty water barrel and settles in the front of the boat. "Chappy in the stern. Ethan's mates, you can row."

With everyone in place, a pirate releases the boat locks and others lower the cockboat by long ropes until it settles into the sea. Jake seizes one oar and Spencer the other. Spencer has brought a bottle from the ship. He balances it carefully between his feet while he rows. The boys settle into a rhythm of rowing that moves the boat quickly toward land.

"Where the heck are we heading?" Jake asks.

"North Carolina," Liz informs him. "We're near Albemarle Sound."

In less than twenty minutes, the bottom of the rowboat crunches on the rocky beach and everyone climbs out.

Ethan has barely stepped from the boat when Chappy shoves him viciously from behind. Stumbling in the frothy waves, Ethan splashes to his hands and knees.

"I told you we weren't finished yet, you jelly-boned sniveler!" the shirtless pirate snarls, his long fingers curved like claws.

Ethan lurches to his feet, but Liz already has her blade out, waving it in warning. "Work before play, boys. After you've filled that barrel, you can spill some blood." A flick of the sword points

them toward a silvery stream trickling from nearby woods and winding across the beach.

Chappy squints at Liz through snake eyes, his hand hovering near his sword hilt. After a moment, he shrugs.

"Let the lass have her way," he says. His voice is calm, but his lizard face is dark with anger and dotted with sweat. "I've no wish to put my sword through a wench."

"Humph," Long Liz grunts. "Let's get that water stowed."

Chappy and the boys wrestle the awkward barrel from the cockboat and roll it up the beach. Using a dagger picked up during the battle with the slave ship, Ethan pries the top from the container and draws a bucket from inside. Taking turns dipping the bucket into the stream, the boys soon fill the barrel. Chappy stands aside scornfully as the work is completed and the lid is pounded in place.

"Hurry up, you duck-kneed barnacle," he barks at Ethan. "The sharks are hungry, and I mean to feed them your carcass."

Without a word, the boys heave the barrel into the boat and return to the beach. Long Liz calls, "I brought the prize along." She pitches Ethan the sword that earned Chappy's hatred. The midday sun glints on the razor edge and the gold hand-guard. Ethan catches it clumsily and holds it uncertainly.

Liz shakes her head with disgust. "I get his hat when he's dead," she tells Jake and Spencer.

"There's no reason for this fight," Ethan says to Chappy. "It's stupid to kill somebody because of a quarrel."

 TURN TO PAGE 109.

## WAR AND PEACE

Jesus taught his followers, "Blessed are the peacemakers, for they will be called children of God." (Matthew 5:9) Jesus also warned that, "All who draw the sword will die by the sword." (Matthew 26:52) Maybe sometimes we have to fight, but nothing good will come from the duel between Ethan and Chappy. It looks like someone is about to die for no reason.

If you want a clue about how the fight will turn out, you can use this verse from the Old Testament book of Ecclesiastes. But this puzzle is a double-trouble brain twister! The letters in each word are jumbled. First, unscramble them. When each word is fixed, put the words in the right order and you'll have the answer. (Hint: Just to help you a little, the first letter of the sentence is capitalized.)

hatn ewopnas fo si tebetr awr iosWdm

---

See answer on page 200.

**F**ine," Ethan snaps at Liz. "Who needs your company? I've met friendlier pit bulls."

Blackbeard shrugs. "Find something to do," he says to the boys. "Everyone pulls his weight on my ship."

The cook grabs Spencer's arm. "The chicken coop needs cleaning, and you're small enough to get in there. Come with me, boy."

A black pirate with bowlegs and wide shoulders seizes Jake's hand and studies his fingers. "Strong, but soft. Let's put callouses on those lady fingers."

He points Jake to a pile of worn and tattered ropes.

"Unravel those old ropes and put the strands in that basket." The bowlegged man squats on the deck and starts tugging ropes apart.

"What a waste of time," Jake moans.

"Knotty-pated barnacle!" snaps the pirate. "We'll mix the hemp fibers with tar, and patch cracks among the timbers. That's what keeps us afloat, worthless lubber."

"We'll see who's worthless," Jake bristles. "I'll fill a basket before you do."

The pirate grins, showing a gold tooth. "The day your satin hands outwork me the sun will rise in the west."

Ethan peers around the ship, looking for a way to pitch in. A surly voice sounds in his ear.

"Mr. Hands told me to put you to work," Chappy Benjamin says, grinning with satisfaction. He chuckles at the expression on Ethan's face. The time traveler's hand moves to the dagger in his belt, a weapon he picked up in the fight on board *Le Lac Noir*. "Don't be afeared. I'll keep my sword tucked in. No fighting on board. Captain's orders, remember?"

The pirate's mockery annoys Ethan, and before he can reconsider the words, he says, "How was the cat o' nine tails?"

Something stirs in the pirate's dark, sly eyes, like a serpent coiling in the shadows. But his smile never flickers. "All in a day's work, mate," he says with a chuckle. He's wearing a shirt now, and he turns so that Ethan can see the bloody fabric clinging to his back. "The cat and me, we're old friends."

The smile vanishing, the pirate thrusts his lizard face close to Ethan and says, "The jardin needs tending. So does the topsail on the main mast. Choose your chore."

IF YOU THINK ETHAN SHOULD TEND THE JARDIN, TURN TO PAGE 113.

IF YOU THINK ETHAN SHOULD CHECK THE TOPSAIL, TURN TO PAGE 121.

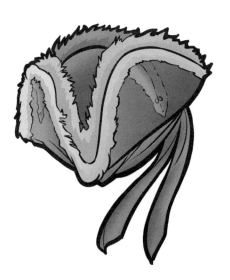

TIME CRASHERS YOU DECIDE

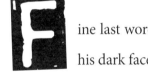ine last words," Chappy says, brushing perspiration from his dark face. "Raise your sword, milk-livered maggot."

Trickles of sweat wind down the pirate's bare chest and back. One stream of sweat seems to be a trail of tears from the eye of the tattooed snake on his neck. His back is torn and bloody from the beating with the cat o' nine tails.

Jake tells Spencer, "He sweats like a boy at his first school dance."

"That's what I'm counting on," Spencer whispers. He lifts the bottle brought from *Queen Anne's Revenge.* In a louder voice, he shouts to Ethan, "It sure is hot out here. Have a long drink of grog before you start."

Ethan aims a quizzical look at his friend. Spencer knows he's not going to drink that mixture of stale water and rum. What is the clever boy planning?

As Spencer extends the grog, Chappy grabs the bottle. "Let a real man drink first," he snarls.

"That's not for you!" Spencer protests. "Don't drink that!"

Yanking the cork with his teeth, the pirate hoists the bottle and guzzles greedily, liquid spilling over his chest. After quenching his thirst, he up-ends the bottle over his head, drenching his shoulders and raw back.

"I tried to warn him," Spencer says, turning away to hide a smile.

Flinging the bottle away, Chappy raises his cutlass. The blade is not as long as Ethan's sword, but the greater weight of the cutlass makes it more powerful. *Clang! Clang!* Each time Ethan lifts his sword, the deadly cutlass smashes it aside. To the left. Now to the right. Chappy isn't much larger than Ethan, but he is a veteran of a hundred fights. The cutlass moves as an extension of the pirate's arm, darting as quickly as a lizard's tongue chasing flies.

Ethan moves constantly backward, giving ground to Chappy's cruel attack. The laughing pirate presses forward again and again.

"You should've left that sword for someone who knows how to use it," he jeers at Ethan.

In minutes, Ethan's arm is exhausted, and it's hard to keep the sword point high. Chappy pretends to chop at Ethan's leg, but when the time traveler lowers his sword in defense, the pirate's swing changes

directions. Chappy hammers the lighter sword so viciously that Ethan's fingers go numb. The time traveler's sword flies from his grip, spins through the sunlight, and thuds into the sand ten feet away. Ethan stands helpless before his enemy.

The pirate chuckles and poises his sword point over Ethan's heart.

Jake and Spencer exchange frightened glances.

 IF YOU THINK ETHAN'S FRIENDS SHOULD JOIN THE FIGHT, TURN TO **PAGE 129**.

 IF YOU THINK THE BOYS SHOULD LEAVE ETHAN TO FIGHT ALONE, TURN TO **PAGE 131**.

"The jardin," Ethan decides.

Despite his mistrust, Ethan wonders about the jardin. He doesn't know the term and he loves learning about life on a pirate ship.

"This way," Chappy grunts.

He pitches Ethan a wooden bucket tied to a long coil of rope. Ethan follows Chappy to the front—the bow—of the *Queen Anne's Revenge*. From the front of the ship, a long, pointed timber extends over the ocean. From his reading, Ethan recognizes this as the bowsprit. Ropes stretching up from the bowsprit connect with the forward mast and hold sails. Another flap of sail cloth, the size of a bedspread, flaps loose beneath the bowsprit.

"Where's the jardin?" Ethan asks as they stand before the bowsprit.

Chappy points downward. Just beneath the bowsprit is a platform surrounded by rails, a small balcony on the front of the ship. The platform is low, hidden from workers on deck. Chappy scrambles down and Ethan follows him with the bucket and rope. A hole is cut in the middle of the platform, just big enough to drop a basketball through. Glancing through the hole, Ethan sees the ocean racing by below.

"The jardin," Chappy sneers.

Ethan realizes this is the ship's toilet. Some of the men probably keep buckets in their cabins which they dump overboard. But for those on duty, this is the handiest toilet. The wood around the jardin is wet and stained. The breeze doesn't quite carry away a familiar stench.

"Some of the boys don't aim so well," Chappy says, "and the Cap'n believes in a tight ship. Lower that bucket over the side and splash this clear. Three times ought to be good enough."

Chappy leans on the head rail. Ethan drops the bucket into the sea, and then hauls the heavy water hand over hand. The rope reddens his palms, and his muscles burn ferociously. When the bucket is in hand, Ethan pours water slowly around the jardin. He takes his time, letting his arms rest before lowering the bucket again.

"Dangerous out here," Chappy muses. "If a man fell over the rail, no one on deck would be the wiser. The prow of the ship would plow him under. A bad way to go."

As Ethan struggles to hoist the second bucket of water, Chappy continues.

"That's a dangerous job, too," he says. "Leaning over the rail like that, pulling on a rope. Easy to lose your balance. Very risky."

Ethan wrestles the second bucketful over the rail and again dumps it on the smelly planks. Chappy smiles wickedly, "One more bucket. Captain's orders."

The pirate turns his back on Ethan, scanning the horizon. "Aye, a dangerous place here at the jardin, but a beautiful view."

Trying to out-guess the vicious pirate, Ethan prepares for the worst. Then he drops the bucket into the frothy sea far below. He feels the jerk as current fills the bucket and begins the task of raising it once more. His muscles are ready to go on strike, and blisters are sprouting on his hands. His belly pressed against the rail, Ethan forces his arms to raise the weight a foot at a time.

Chappy leans over him, peering down at the waves.

"Say hello to Davy Jones," he breathes in Ethan's ear.

Suddenly Chappy grips Ethan's belt and hoists him over the head rail. With a violent push, the time traveler is flung into space. Sky above and sea beneath, Ethan spins through the air. Panic kicks the breath from his lungs, but he hangs on to the bucket rope. For a heartbeat, the rope flops in the air like a snake, but then the line grows tight. Ethan bites back a cry at the pain in his raw hands and clings to the rope with every ounce of will. His grip holds. Dangling from the rope, he bangs into the prow of the ship, fifteen feet below the jardin platform.

Chappy stares in shock, his eyes bugging like a chameleon. In seconds he figures out how Ethan saved himself. While Chappy was looking away, Ethan tied the free end of the rope to the head rail. The double knot fastens one end of the rope to the rail, while Ethan clings for dear life. A crooked grin exposes Chappy's yellow teeth.

"I lied about keeping my sword in my belt," he calls. Laying the edge of his cutlass on the thick knot, he saws at the hemp strands. Ethan clinches the rope between his knees and climbs. The rope, slippery with sea water and Ethan's blood, slides through his grip. For each foot he rises, he slides six inches downward. The nearness of death drives from his mind all thoughts of blistered flesh and throbbing muscles.

*Climb!* he orders himself. Abs lift, knees clinch, hands claw upward. *Climb!*

Ethan looks up. Triumph shines on Chappy's gloating face as the rope parts strand by strand beneath the edge of his blade.

But Chappy isn't alone.

On the deck above the platform, a tall, bearded figure glares down, taking careful aim with a flintlock pistol. The gun bangs with a puff of smoke. The pistol ball smashes into Chappy's right shoulder, and the pirate pitches forward over the head rail. His smug expression turns to terror. He falls past Ethan, a groping hand brushing the boy's sleeve. He hits the sea and the frothy water sucks him beneath the *Queen Anne's Revenge.*

Blackbeard leaps down to the jardin with a thump of heavy boots. He offers no help as Ethan struggles up the rope and painfully hauls himself over the rail. Ethan collapses on the rough planks at the pirate captain's feet.

"Bad for discipline when crewmen start killing each other," Blackbeard says matter-of-factly. As he walks away, he calls over his shoulder, "On my ship, I'm the one that does the killing."

Although his legs feel as if the bones have been replaced with over-cooked spaghetti, Ethan clambers from the bowsprit and onto the main deck. He makes his way to the main mast and slumps to the deck with his back to the spar.

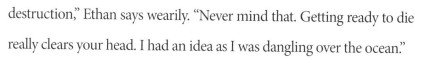

"We heard a gun," Jake says, settling beside Ethan.

"What happened?" Spencer asks, squatting next to Jake.

"More death and destruction," Ethan says wearily. "Never mind that. Getting ready to die really clears your head. I had an idea as I was dangling over the ocean."

His friends lean in close as Ethan continues.

"We've been thinking that the retrieval pulse is tied to a *place*. But what if it's actually tied to a *thing?*"

"A thing?" Jake repeats, cocking his head in confusion. Suddenly his eyes brighten. "Like that platform on top of the main mast!"

Ethan nods.

"Hmmm …" Spencer muses, stroking his chin in thought. "Instead of a spatio-chronal nexus …"

"If your mouth is big enough for words like that," Jake says, "it's probably big enough for a triple-decker fist sandwich. No more Spock talk."

"What do you think, Spence?" Ethan asks. "Could that platform be our ride home?"

The genius stares into the distance for several minutes.

"Okay," Spencer says. "In words even Jake can understand." He leans toward the athlete and pronounces the words slowly and carefully. "It. Might. Work."

Jake lifts one hand and Spencer slaps it in a noisy high five.

"In other words," Ethan presses on, ignoring his friends' clowning, "if I'm right, we don't have to find some invisible, impossible spot in the middle of the ocean. We can catch the next retrieval pulse on top of the main mast."

"In less than an hour, if my calculations are on target," Spencer says.

 TURN TO **PAGE 135**.

than itches to climb the main mast. When he was there before, it was too stormy for him to enjoy the experience.

"Let's take a look at the main sail," he says to Chappy.

The pirate tips his head to stare at the top of the tall, central mast. "Are you brave or stupid?" he wonders.

There are three masts on the *Queen Anne's Revenge*—tall, timber spars that carry the weight of the sails. The mast near the front of the ship is the fore mast; the mizzen mast is at the back or stern of the ship. In the middle is the tallest of all, the main mast rising nearly a hundred feet above the deck. A human body falling from that height would hit the deck at a speed of 90 miles per hour. At least, that's what Spencer had explained as they wandered the ship. Even smacking the ocean at that speed might mean a trip to the emergency room. Ethan reminds himself that it's a long trip to the nearest emergency room, about four hundred years long.

With a hearty laugh, the pirate slaps him on the back. The blow is too hard to be friendly. "Trust ol' Chappy to take care of you," he says, grinning a serpent smile. "I'll watch over you like your mama."

"What do we have to do?" Ethan asks when they stand at the foot of the great mast.

"The bosun wants us to check the rigging," Chappy explains. "He says it feels sluggish."

Ethan nods. He knows the rigging is the complicated web of ropes that raises and lowers the sails.

"Get moving," Chappy orders. "I ain't hauling your carcass up there, your majesty."

Ethan stares up at the soaring mast. A platform waits about one-third of the way to the top. A web of taut ropes makes a kind of shaky ladder to the platform.

"Hit those ratlines, you mewling whey-face," Chappy barks. "Those sails won't come to us; we gotta go to them."

Ethan starts up the vibrating ropes. Each time he lifts a foot or shifts his hold, the ratlines shake and sway under his weight. The climbing is much harder than ascending a wooden ladder. After only a few yards, the coarse lines rub the skin from his hands, leaving his palms sore and raw.

Crowding Ethan, Chappy follows him up. The pirate seems as much at home on the ratlines as Jake would be on a football field or Spencer in a library.

"My granny can outclimb you," Chappy sings out loud enough for half the crew to hear him. "And she has two peg legs."

Laughter floats up from the deck, and Ethan's face reddens to match his blistering hands. Feeling as awkward as a nine-legged spider, Ethan works his way unsteadily to the first platform on the main mast. Chappy leaps nimbly to stand beside him. Ethan is annoyed by how easy the sailor makes it look. At this height, Ethan and Chappy are between two of the three sails on the mainmast. The pirate examines the stretch of fabric spread beneath them, and tugs ropes here and there. Wind bellies the thick canvas.

Ethan has heard tales of sail makers who could break walnuts between their fingers. As he strokes the heavy sailcloth, he believes the stories might be true. He is in awe of the craftsmen who wield long needles to stitch or repair this material. The fabric is woven from cotton, linen, and hemp. It has to be extremely strong to bear the winds that drive the ship. From his reading, Ethan estimates the weight of *Queen Anne's Revenge* at about 300 tons. The movement of that massive bulk, well over half a million pounds, depends on the strength of the sails.

Chappy satisfies himself with the condition of the lower sail, and he turns his attention to the middle sail overhead. Again, he eyes the sail itself as well as the ropes that raise, lower, and fasten it. After a few minutes, he says, "Keep climbing, unless you've no belly for it."

Another set of ratlines leads to the next platform two-thirds of the way up the mast. Although Chappy bullies and mocks him on the ascent, Ethan feels he's getting the hang of moving up the rope webs. He wishes for tougher hands, but his balance and movements are better. What had Liz called him when they first met? A drunken, peg-legged monkey? He wishes she were here to see him now.

After a few minutes on the second platform, Chappy insists they go higher still. The highest platform on the main mast is barely big enough for Chappy and Ethan to stand side-by-side. The wind is stronger at this height. The swaying of the ship, barely noticeable on deck, is greater here. Ethan feels like an ant riding on the tip of an old-fashioned car antenna. He is reassured when the unpredictable wind suddenly drops to a faint breath. The swaying continues, but the great sails settle into limp folds.

"It's a long way down," Chappy observes, yellow teeth bared in a taunting grin. "A man who fell from here would splatter on the deck like a cackle-fruit. They'd have to scoop you up with a chum-bucket."

Ethan notices that Chappy has hooked his ankle into a rope with some slack. Twisting his foot, he loops the line twice around his ankle. Ethan follows suit, wrapping another rope around his own ankle.

"Look at you," Chappy teases. "You're on the line like a real seaman. Nobody can say that ol' Chappy hasn't shown you the ropes."

Chappy's hand lashes out as fast as a striking viper. He grabs Ethan's wrist in a vice-like hold and yanks the boy's right hand free from the mast. Hooking the mast with one leg, Chappy uses his other hand to peel the fingers of Ethan's left hand from the timber. Ethan fights, but Chappy's grip is overpowering. Years of hoisting sail and running lines have made his hands steely strong.

Chappy leans forward, nose to nose with Ethan. His breath reeks of fish and ale. "I warned you that I'd settle up with you later," he snarls. "Later is now."

Without another word, the vicious pirate pushes Ethan off the platform. For a moment the Time Crasher flails in the air, then the rope around his ankle grabs tight. Hanging upside-down, Ethan winces, wondering if his foot will be jerked from his leg. From Ethan's position the world goes topsy-turvy, the deck far above and the sky distant below. Figures on the deck stare with upturned faces and point at his plight.

"Don't worry!" Chappy shouts, hoping to be heard below. "I'll save you!" In a lower voice, he growls at Ethan, "Get ready to make a big splash, hornswoggler. You'll have no use for that fancy sword when your face meets the deck."

With one hand clutching the mast, Chappy reaches for Ethan's leg. From below it looks like he's hauling the helpless boy back on the platform. In fact, he twists at the rope, trying to jerk it free from Ethan's leg and send him plummeting head-first. Ethan kicks desperately with his free foot. His heel slams Chappy's fumbling fingers. Bones crack.

"You stinking cullion!" Chappy wails.

The enraged pirate shakes his foot free from the safety rope and steps carefully down onto the yard—the long, wooden spar that runs along the top edge of the sail. Sitting on the yard, he scoots his bottom along until he gets within reach of Ethan. Leaning way out, Chappy gropes for the rope from which the time traveler is hanging. Straining, his fingers are only inches away from Ethan's lifeline when a sudden gust of high wind fills the sail. The canvas cloth snaps tight and billows outward.

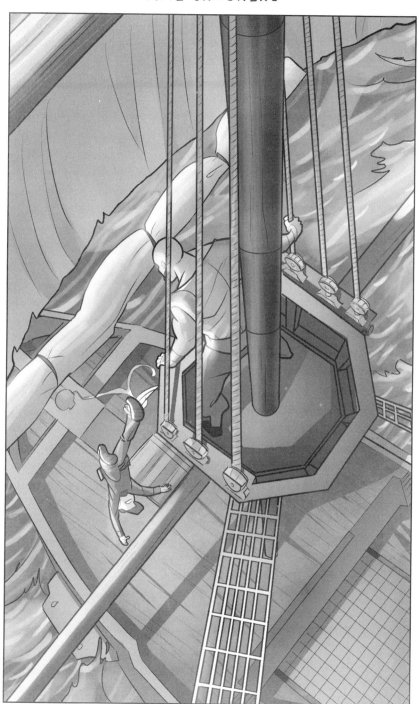

Chappy, already off balance and overreaching, is caught off guard. The fabric balloons and punches his legs outward. He wobbles on the yard, groping with his wounded hand for a grip. But the broken fingers fail him. With a wild screech of fear and anger, Chappy slips from the yard. A desperate kick against the sailcloth sends him flying well beyond the deck and he hits the sea with a terrible smack.

Even high in the air, Ethan can hear Blackbeard's disgusted voice. "Leave him for the fishies," he orders. "Even if he's alive, there's no room on the *Queen Anne's Revenge* for a seaman who can't keep his balance on a yard."

Ethan pushes his aching muscles to the limit. He jackknifes his body and grabs the safety rope with blistered hands. Hand over hand, he pulls himself upright and scrambles back onto the platform. After a moment to catch his breath, he makes the climb down the ratlines. On deck, he sinks to the planks and rests his back against the mast.

 TURN TO **PAGE 133.**

I can't stand here while he kills my best friend," Jake says. The athlete snatches up Ethan's lost sword and yells at Chappy. "You beat him! That's enough!"

"Boy, don't stick your nose where it might get sliced off," Chappy snarls. "It's over when his body is floating ..." He breaks off, his expression confused. The pirate blinks rapidly and wipes sweat from his forehead. He finishes the sentence, panting between words. "When his body—is floating—on the—tide."

A shiver shakes his body. The sweat streaming down his face is joined by a trickle of spit from the corner of his mouth. The heavy cutlass drops from his trembling hand.

"What?" the tattooed man asks, staggering. "What is ...?"

Dropping his own sword, Jake catches the falling pirate in strong arms and lowers him to the sandy earth.

"I guess it worked," Spencer says, smiling smugly.

 TURN TO PAGE 136.

"Wait!" Spencer urges Jake. "Just another minute or two."

Chappy prods Ethan's chest gently with the cutlass. "I'm deciding whether to kill you quick or slow. Slow is more fun, but it's so hot here."

The pirate sweats even more heavily than before, water streaming from the blunt tip of his flat nose. He shakes his head in confusion and his eyes lose focus for a moment. The outstretched sword trembles in his hand, the point wavering.

"So hot," Chappy says, his words slurring. He takes a step back from Ethan. Raising a dirty finger, he pokes his upper lip and cheek. "Can't feel my face," he mumbles in wonder. The point of the heavy cutlass drops to the sand.

Ethan doesn't understand what's happening, but he grabs the

weapon and peels the pirate's clammy fingers from the handle.

"The fight's over, Chappy!" Ethan declares. "You lost."

Chappy nods uncertainly.

"'Y' beat me," he mumbles. "Beaten by a scurvy ..."

The insult is left unfinished as Chappy sinks to his knees and topples face forward on the beach.

Spencer strides forward and peers curiously at the fallen man. "I guess it worked," he says in satisfaction.

 TURN TO **PAGE 136**.

**S**pencer and Jake settle beside Ethan, concern on their faces.

"Spill it," Jake says. "What happened with you and Chappy?"

Ethan shakes his head wearily. "Life is cheap on a pirate ship. I want to go home."

"That's not going to happen," Spencer says gently.

"I think you're wrong," Ethan says.

"Spencer wrong?" Jake exclaims. "Wow! Front page story: MEGA GENIUS SCREWS UP!"

"Just as I started down the mast, I ... felt something," Ethan confides. "It was a tingle in my gut and a strange buzz along my spine."

"*The retrieval pulse?*" Spencer asks, mouth gaping. "The beam that will take us back to our own time?"

Ethan nods. "It faded as I climbed down the ratlines."

"The removal bus is going to pick us up on the platform at the top of the mast?" Jake asks.

"Retrieval pulse!" Spencer corrects him. "That would mean that the pulse is tied to a *thing* instead of a *place*. If the machine creates a five-dimensional construct in four-dimensional reality, we could postulate—"

Jake interrupts. "Spence, old buddy, just once try to be a normal person. Just say, 'Wow! That's great news.'"

"That's an extremely fortuitous revelation," Spencer declares to Ethan. He turns to Jake and adds, "How was that?"

Jake rolls his eyes. "Oh, yeah. That was 100% normal."

"In other words," Ethan presses on, ignoring his friends' clowning, "we don't have to find some spot in midair out in the middle of the ocean. We just have to get to the top of the main mast on schedule."

"In about fifty minutes by my calculations," Spencer says.

CONTINUE TO **PAGE 135.**

**S**o we meet here in half an hour, scamper up the pole, and sayonara *Queen Anne's Revenge*," Jake says. He reaches into his multi-pocketed vest, pulls out a small tube, and pitches it to Ethan. "Aloe cream. After you smear it on, tie bandanas around your palms."

The weather changes dramatically in the next thirty minutes. The wind shifts direction, the temperature drops, and low clouds fill the sky. An occasional rumble of thunder rolls across the choppy sea as the boys gather at the main mast.

 TURN TO **PAGE 172.**

W hat's the matter with him?" Ethan asks his brainy friend.

"Tetrodotoxin," Spencer says. "TTX for short."

"Try it in English, Brain Boy," Jake grunts.

"Fish guts," Spencer explains, "from a puffer fish."

"Is that the one you grabbed when the barrel of salted fish broke on the deck?" Ethan asks, recalling his friend's odd behavior when the food was moved from the slave ship to *Queen Anne's Revenge*.

Spencer nods. "Somebody must have netted it by mistake and thrown it in with the other fish. The meat and organs contain a very powerful chemical."

"Retro-concoction," Jake says.

"Uh, close enough," Spencer agrees. "I thought the puffer fish might come in handy so I stashed it away wrapped in a rag. When I knew the duel between Chappy and Ethan was coming, I pushed some pieces of puffer fish into a bottle of grog. The TTX dissolved into the alcohol. Then all I had to do was trick the bully into drinking it."

"What's going to happen to him?" Ethan asks.

"Headache, chills, vomiting …" Spencer begins.

Chappy gags violently.

"Right on schedule," Spencer says. "His body is getting rid of the poison."

Spencer retrieves the bucket from the dinghy and fills it with water. He pours it over Chappy's wounded back. "That should help. The TTX also enters the body through skin and open sores. It was lucky when he dumped the rest of the grog over his shoulders. That made the chemical go to work much faster."

"So he's not going to die," Ethan says with relief.

"What do you care?" Long Liz asks. "He would have hacked you into shark bait."

"Just because Chappy's a killer doesn't mean I have to be one, too," Ethan answers.

Liz reaches out a delicate hand

and fingers the small cross that hangs around Ethan's neck. "Do your friends believe the way you do?"

Ethan nods.

"Then maybe I can trust you," she says. "I need help, and I have no one else to turn to."

From a pocket, she produces a folded piece of leather and opens it. The lines of a faded map are visible in the afternoon sun.

 TURN TO **PAGE 140**.

# TREASURE HUNTING

Maybe you're never going to find a chest of buried pirate loot, but an even better treasure is waiting for you if you're willing to hunt for it. What's the treasure? How can you find it? Here's a message from God, but you'll have to do some hunting and seeking. Find—and scratch out—each B and G and P and J and Q in the letters below. When you've gotten rid of those letters, you'll be able to read God's message about treasure hunting.

B Y O P U W I J L P L S E G B E K M B E A N Q D F I J N D M E P

G W P H B E N P Y O P U S E J G E K Q M E P B

Q W G I T P J P H G A L J L Y O Q U P R G H E B J A R P T.

See answers on page 200.

That looks like the peninsula we're standing on," Ethan says, tapping the map.

"Aye," Liz agrees. "We're here." Her finger pokes the leather. "And I mean to reach this spot." Her fingertip slides to two letters inked on the map—an elaborate, entwining W and K.

"A treasure map?" Jake asks.

"That's a myth," Spencer corrects him. "Your average pirate wasn't planning for retirement. They spent their money drinking and gambling whenever they landed in port. Pirates didn't really bury treasure."

"Except for William Kidd," Ethan says, indicating the initials on the leather map. "Commanding the *Adventure Galley*, Captain Kidd looted over seven million dollars of gold and silver from the

# TIME CRASHERS

*Quedagh Merchant* in 1698. Expecting to be arrested, Kidd hid treasure in several different places on Gardiner's Island. He hoped to use the money as a bribe in case he was brought to trial."

"Did his plan work?" Jake asks.

Long Liz laughs harshly. "They hanged him in London."

"Twice. The rope broke the first time." Ethan looks at Liz skeptically.

"All of Kidd's hidden treasure on Gardiner's Island was recovered."

"True," Liz agrees, "but not all of it was hidden on that island. One chest is buried on this peninsula."

"How did you get the map?" Ethan asks.

"I gave a drink of water to a dying man in a Port Royale alley," Liz says, a faraway look in her eyes. "He shoved the map into my hands. He claimed he won it in a dice game with Able Owens, one of Kidd's sailors."

"You believe him?" Spencer asks.

"I want to believe him," Liz admits. "I've sailed with Blackbeard nearly a year waiting for an opportunity to test this map."

"We'll help you find the treasure," Ethan says.

"What about Chappy?" Jake asks.

"He'll be out of it for hours," Spencer assures them. "We can leave him to rest."

Ethan studies the map and suggests two possible routes. "The treasure is due north on the other side of this thick forest. We'll make better time if we skirt the woods. So do we take the western path around the trees or head east along the coast?"

IF YOU THINK THE GROUP SHOULD TRAVEL EAST, CONTINUE TO **PAGE 144**.

IF YOU THINK THEY SHOULD TRAVEL WEST, TURN TO **PAGE 150**.

**E**ast," Liz decides. "I like the sound of the sea."

The little band sets off along the beach. At first the going is easy, but the coastline soon grows rocky. As the tide rises, they head inland where the land is marshy and the air hums with mosquitoes.

Jake stops suddenly beside a wide stream choked with reeds and cattails. He points to a hummock of dry land where a red, yellow, and black snake is sunning. "Coral snake!" he warns. "Those things are poisonous!"

"Wrong and wrong again," Spencer says. "First, coral snakes are not poisonous; they are venomous. Second, that's not a coral snake. It's a scarlet king snake. Notice how the red and black stripes meet. Remember the old rhyme: Red next to yellow will kill a fellow; red next to black is a friend to Jack."

"That's a relief," Jake says. Although the athlete is ready for almost any danger, snakes turn his legs weak and his heart faint.

"Not so much," Spencer disagrees. "The snake isn't a problem, but see that log floating next to the path?"

"Yeah," Jake says. "So what?"

"It's not a log," Spencer says. "It's an alligator."

"And a big one," Ethan says in awe. "That guy must be fifteen feet long."

"We can't go back to the beach," Liz laments. "The tide is too high. We have to find a way past the brute."

"I wish we had some rope," Spencer says.

"I've got fishing line in my vest," Jake offers, but Spencer shakes his head.

"We need something easier to handle," he says.

"I carry rope," Liz informs them.

They look the girl up and down from her three-cornered hat to the leather boots. She grins and unties the knot cinching a red sash around her waist. The red fabric unwraps several times until the pirate is holding a length of red fabric almost twenty feet long.

"It's silk," Liz says, "light but strong."

"Perfect," Spencer says. He takes the sash and ties an overhand knot in the middle, loose and open like a lasso. He hands one end of the red fabric to Ethan and the other end to Jake. "It's an alligator trap," he tells his friends. "Yank it tight when the gator puts his head through. Catch the middle of his snout. That's important so you can hold his mouth shut."

"No way this little rag is gonna shut that monster's mouth," Jake says. "I read that an alligator has the strongest bite in nature. Stronger than a shark or a lion."

"That's true," Spencer agrees, "but their jaws have very little *opening* power. You could easily tie a gator's mouth shut with twine."

"Yeah, if his tail didn't break your legs and his claws didn't rip open your belly," Jake adds.

"That's why I'm trusting you guys to hold on very tight," Spencer urges.

The boys lay the red sash across the ground with the open noose spread wide. Spencer positions himself on the other side of the sash and claps his hands to get the gator's attention. "Here I am," he calls.

"Come and get it! Dinner time!"

With shocking speed, the alligator bolts from the water and lurches toward Spencer. Even Spencer is startled. He leaps backward, slipping on the muddy ground. But Ethan and Jake have lifted the red rope. As the swamp killer lunges forward, its nose enters the noose and the boys yank the silk trap with all their might. The red band closes like a clamp on the snout of the unsuspecting reptile. The angry gator shakes his head from side to side, but Ethan and Jake strain to hold him in place.

"Whoa!" Jake shouts. "This leathery lizard is strong!"

The alligator turns his head toward Jake. Ethan struggles to hold him back, his heels skidding in the muck. Now the predator tries to reach Ethan, and it's Jake's turn to strain against the pull.

"Move!" Spencer shouts at Long Liz. The pirate leaps over the thrashing gator, followed by Spencer on her heels.

The enraged reptile backs into the water, still struggling against the sash. His frantic tail lashes the green water into foam.

"That's our cue," Jake calls. He and Ethan release the red sash and sprint past the armored monster. He doesn't notice them pass. He is intent on rubbing his long snout on the bank, loosening the silk trap. As the little group look back, catching their breath, the red binding slips loose and the gator snaps his jaws furiously.

"Liz, we'll wait if you want to go back for your belt," Ethan says innocently.

"I've got another just like it in my cabin on the ship," Liz says, shuddering. "Let's hope we don't run into him on our way back."

TURN TO **PAGE 157**.

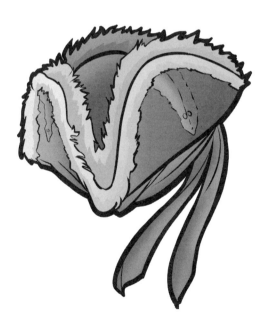

W est," Spencer insists. "Anything to get away from the sound of the ocean."

The land climbs gently from the shore, then drops again. The treasure seekers keep the woods to their right, and slog through salty marsh land. Dragonflies dart like green fairies and the buzz of insects drowns out any sound from the waves a few miles away. At first, they try to hop from one bit of solid land to another, but soon they are soaked with green water and their legs are crusted with gray muck.

Liz glares at Spencer and asks, "Whose idea was it to come this way?"

"I make a mistake now and then just to remember what it feels like," Spencer says, brushing a mosquito from his nose.

Ethan is relieved that his straight-A buddy is getting back to his old self, shaking off the disappointment of being stranded in the past. But Ethan can't quite believe there's no way for them to return to their own time. Spencer is almost always right, but something feels wrong to Ethan. Something about the design of the time machine ...

His thinking is interrupted by a cry from Long Liz.

"A pox on this stinking swamp," she erupts. She has sunk into sludge up to her chest. "I can't get my feet on anything solid."

The boys slog to her aid, but as they try to pull her free, each boy is himself sucked into the stinking mire. In seconds, all four are struggling against the sucking ooze. The more they thrash and fight, the faster they sink. The sludge rises to their armpits, then to their chins.

"Stop moving!" Spencer shouts. "Freeze!"

Everyone obeys. The only movement is a dragonfly swooping low to examine the trapped youngsters.

"We've stumbled into a colloid hydrogel," Spencer explains. "When dealing with a non-Newtonian liquid, the preferred course of action—"

"Gimme the idiot's version," Jake pleads.

"Quicksand," Spencer says. "There's probably a spring beneath us. The upward push of the water causes sand, clay, and silt to float in a thick soup."

"It doesn't taste like soup," Liz mutters.

"What now?" Ethan asks.

"Wiggle your legs very slowly," Spencer instructs them. "Extend your arms and try to get your body spread out on the surface."

After a moment, Liz says, "It's working. I'm floating to the top."

"Not for me," Jake wails, spitting out filthy water. "I'm sinking deeper."

"Plan B," Spencer says. He tries to keep his voice even, but a hint of panic creeps in. "Jake, you're the heaviest. The supplies stuffed in your pockets add to the weight. You stop moving. Be a statue, buddy."

"Got it," Jake agrees.

"Liz, you're the lightest of us," Spencer says. "Spread your body on the surface and use your arms to swim toward that fallen tree."

"But Jake's in the way," Liz protests.

"We'll worry about that when you get closer," Spencer says.

Looking like a giant frog, Liz strokes across the quicksand in slow motion. She moves at turtle speed, panting as she inches across the mire. Ethan watches in admiration, knowing her muscles are on fire.

Just the effort to hold her face above the goop must be exhausting.

Jake is sinking even deeper in the ooze, the slime reaching his lower lip.

"Jake, stop wiggling!" Spencer orders.

"I'm searching my pockets," Jake says, tilting back his head.

"Okay," Liz says breathlessly as she reaches Jake.

"Now you're going to climb over Jake to reach the tree," Spencer says. "He's your walkway. You should be able to move quickly for these last few feet."

"He'll sink if I step on him!" Liz objects.

"Maybe not," Jake says. He holds up one hand triumphantly. "Personal flotation device!"

Putting his hand to his lips, he blows steadily and a red balloon appears in his muddy grip. He inflates it to the size of a basketball. "Fingers too slimy to tie it," he pants. "Have to pinch it shut."

"Okay, pirate girl. Save the day." Jake wraps his arms around the balloon. He takes a deep breath.

Liz places her hands on the athlete's shoulders and hoists herself partially above the quicksand. Jake's head goes under the ooze. The pirate struggles to get her knees on Jake's submerged shoulders, then stands shakily, almost as if she is walking on water. Her boots, planted on shoulders of the sunken time traveler, are shin deep in the mire. Crouching slightly, she leaps for the fallen tree. Her outstretched fingers brush a limb, slide off, and then her other hand finds a grip. She scrambles onto the horizontal trunk.

The pirate turns anxiously toward Jake, hoping to see him bob to the surface. Instead a great bubble of air belches from the quicksand.

"The balloon burst," Spencer moans.

Liz whips a sword from her belt and hacks a limb from the dead tree. The bursting bubble has left a ring of slow circles on the thick surface of the quicksand. Leaning out from her perch, Liz jams the tree limb into the center of the ripples.

Nothing.

She pushes the branch deeper, slowly swirling it around.

"Come on, Jake," Ethan pleads. *God, don't let this be the end.*

A string of smaller bubbles pop on the surface.

Ethan knows Jake has released his breath.

Suddenly, Liz nearly tumbles into the quicksand as the tree limb yanks against her grip. A hand breaks the surface, grabs the slimy wood. Another hand follows, reaching higher on the life-saving branch. A mud-crusted head emerges, sputtering and gasping.

Liz helps the weary Jake wrap his arms around the tree trunk, while Ethan and Spencer shout encouragement. Chest heaving, eyes blinded by mud, Jake gives his friends a shaky thumbs up.

"Biggest fish I ever caught," Liz quips. "But I don't have a skillet big enough to fry it."

Ethan and Spencer begin their own slow swim to safety. Liz unwinds the long red sash around her waist. When each boy gets close enough, she throws out one end of the strong silk fabric, and tows them to the fallen tree.

As they rest their aching muscles, Ethan says, "Jake, when your head popped up, I thought we'd wandered into a monster movie."

"Yeah, *The Football Captain from the Black Lagoon*," Spencer adds.

"I thought it was an improvement over his usual face," Liz says without cracking a smile.

"I'm starting to wish you hadn't rescued me," Jake sighs, digging muck from his ear.

 CONTINUE TO **PAGE 157**.

The rest of the trip is free from danger. Consulting the map often, the four treasure hunters press through boggy country, keeping the dense woods in sight. The trees soon thin into scraggly outliers and the land funnels into a narrow valley. Not far inside the mouth of the valley is a single boulder the size of an elephant. Near the boulder is a small house with smoke drifting from the chimney. Chickens cluck and peck in the yard. Beyond the house, the valley floor is plowed and planted with corn.

A man in work clothes trudges from the field. He greets the little group with a cheery smile as they meet beside the boulder.

"Let me guess," the man says amiably, "you're looking for hidden treasure."

Ethan knows that the shock he sees on his friends' faces must be mirrored in his own expression.

"You beat us to it," Liz accuses him.

"Not exactly," the farmer says.

He introduces himself as Boaz Owens and invites them for dinner. Seated at a plank table in his modest home, the travelers dig into plates of fried corn mush and brown beans. As the guests eat, Boaz Owens asks, "Which one of you has the map?"

Liz eyes him suspiciously. "I do," she admits.

"And you got it from Able Owens, one of Captain Kidd's officers, right?" the farmer asks gently.

"Not directly, but yes, the map came from him," Liz agrees.

"What of it?"

"Able Owens and Boaz Owens," Ethan says. "Are you related?"

"Uncle Able is the black sheep in our family," the farmer says. "He visited here once and found my farm a dreadfully lonely place. When he left, he promised he'd send a visitor now and then." Boaz Owens took a bite of beans and chewed contentedly. "He kept that promise."

Liz sputters, "You mean the map is—"

"A fake," Boaz agrees. "It's well known that Uncle Able sailed with Kidd. When he needs quick money or a stake for a card game, my uncle draws up a map and passes it off on some lackwit."

Liz turns scarlet.

"How many times have people come here looking for Kidd's hidden gold?" Ethan asks.

"I'll show you," Boaz says, rising from his bench at the table. As he leads them outside, the farmer picks up an iron spike from a shelf near the door.

They stroll to the boulder a hundred yards from the house. The farmer places the spike's point against the limestone and moves it up and down. The iron digs into the stone, carving a line as long a man's finger. When the carving is deep enough, Boaz leans over and blows it clean of dust. Beside it are seven matching lines.

"You're number eight," he says, admiring his handiwork.

"Then there's no treasure buried in the ground," Liz says bitterly.

"I wouldn't say that," Boaz exclaims, sweeping a hand toward the shoulder-high corn stalks in his field. "Rich bottom land. The best treasure a man could hope for."

The angry expression on Liz's face softens as she surveys the rows of growing green. She sighs. Ethan wonders if there is a good reason to return to Blackbeard and the pirates. That life is bloody and violent. This life is peaceful and worthwhile.

 IF YOU THINK THE TIME CRASHERS SHOULD STAY WITH FARMER OWENS, CONTINUE TO **PAGE 161**.

 IF YOU THINK THE BOYS SHOULD RETURN TO QUEEN ANNE'S REVENGE, TURN TO **PAGE 163**.

r. Owens," Ethan asks impulsively, "is there room here for others who might want to settle?"

Boaz doesn't seem surprised by the question.

"Oh, yes," he says. "There's far more land here than I can plow. You could stay with me until we build you a place. If you've the knack for hunting, there's rabbit and squirrel in the woods. I hear alligator is tasty. And I wouldn't mind a neighbor for a nightly chess match."

"What about it?" Ethan asks his friends. "I'm not cut out for stabbing people. If we're stuck here anyway, this wouldn't be a bad life."

Spencer shrugs. "It wouldn't have to be forever, right? If it didn't work, we could head for town."

"Sure," Ethan agrees. "What about you, Jake?"

The athlete grins. "I don't know about farming, but I'd love to try my hand at gator hunting."

"Liz, you can stay, too," Ethan coaxes. "Why do you need buried treasure?"

Liz laughs. "I was going to use the money to buy a home in the country and raise a garden."

Ethan offers his hand to Boaz Owens.

"We'll give it a try," he tells the farmer.

# THE END

YOU DON'T LIKE THIS ENDING?
DO YOU WISH THE TIME CRASHERS HAD MADE OTHER
CHOICES? GOOD NEWS! YOU HAVE A TIME MACHINE.
GO BACK AND DO IT DIFFERENTLY.

THE FINAL ENDING IS UP TO YOU.

E than pushes the wishful thought from his mind. What right do they have to ask for a place with this farmer who has worked so hard to build a productive life?

"We'd best be back to *Queen Anne's Revenge* before nightfall," Liz says.

"Will you be keeping the map?" Boaz asks her.

"It's no use to me now," she says, tugging the damp leather from a grimy pocket. She pitches it to the farmer.

"Thanks," he said. "I have a collection."

"Can you imagine what that map would bring in an online auction?" Spencer muses as they leave the farm behind.

 TURN TO **PAGE 165**.

## DOLLARS AND SENSE

Pirates were so greedy they were willing to threaten, rob, and even murder for money. Is money a bad thing? Of course not, but we must be careful how we feel about money. To read this money message, change each number into a letter. 4 is D, the fourth letter of the alphabet. 10 is J, the tenth letter of the alphabet, and so on. If you have trouble with the number code, you can look up the passage in your Bible.

11-5-5-16-25-15-21-18-12-9-22-5-19-6-18-5-5-
6-18-15-13-20-8-5-12-15-22-5-15-6-13-15-14-
5-25-1-14-4-2-5-3-15-14-20-5-14-20-23-9-20-8-
23-8-1-20-25-15-21-8-1-22-5. (Hebrews 13:5)

See answers on page 200.

Unwilling to face the swampy lowlands a second time, the disappointed treasure seekers hike directly through the forest. In places the brush is thick, and they have to watch for sinkholes, but everyone agrees the woods offer a better path than the bogs or the beach. Even when a brief summer storm sweeps through, they make good time in the shelter of the trees. When they reach the beach, the cockboat is where they left it, but Chappy Benjamin has vanished.

"He can't go back to *Queen Anne's Revenge* and admit that a lubber like Ethan bested him," Liz says without surprise. "Blackbeard has no patience for losers. Chappy will head inland and make his way to the nearest port. Maybe he's wading through the swamp right now." With a wicked smile, she adds, "I hope he doesn't run into trouble."

After washing in the nearby stream, they shove the rowboat into the waves. Spencer and Jake again claim the oars. As they bounce through the waves, Ethan says to Liz, "Sorry about the treasure. What would you have done with the gold?"

Liz removes her tri-corner hat, loosens her hair, and shakes the strands over her shoulders. She says, "I'm good with a blade, but sooner or later I'll meet someone better. Then they'll heave my bloody carcass off the deck and send me to Davy Jones' locker."

The breeze catches her hair and blows it around her face, making her look younger.

"I'd rather die gray-headed in a bed on my own farm," she says wistfully. "I need gold to buy that country estate."

"But the map was bogus," Ethan reminds her. "Now what?"

"I can take care of myself," she says brusquely. Liz turns away toward the prow and ends the conversation.

Ethan scoots closer to Spencer and Jake and lowers his voice.

"I've been thinking about our ..." He glances at Liz who seems to be ignoring them. "Our problem. Dad would never set up the time machine to drop a traveler someplace random. It's too dangerous.

What if you appeared in midair over the Grand Canyon?"

"Wile E. Coyote," Jake says, rowing smoothly. "Splatville."

"And what about water?" Ethan continues. "Most of the world is covered in water, right?"

"About 70 percent," Spencer agrees.

"So if the machine just plops us down at random, seven out of ten times we'd end up in the middle of an ocean," Ethan points out.

"An hour is a long time to tread water waiting for the removal bus," Jake says.

"Retrieval pulse!" Spencer corrects, but his eyes are gleaming. "You're saying your Dad would have programmed the time machine to land us someplace safe. But you can't deny we did appear in midair last night."

"No, we didn't," Ethan argues. "We appeared on the platform of the main mast. We've been thinking the retrieval pulse is tied to a *place*. But what if it's tied to a *thing*?"

"Like the high cross near Lindisfarne," Jake agrees.

"Or the olive tree outside of Pompeii," Ethan says excitedly.

"The olive tree burned up," Spencer points out.

"The stump was still there," Jake says. "Maybe that was enough for the removal bus to grab."

"Let me see if I have this straight," Spencer says. "When the time machine sends us into the past, it locks on some object to make sure we have a safe landing. That object becomes the anchor for the retrieval pulse. When we're ready to go home, we have to be near that object when the pulse activates."

Ethan nods.

"So to return home from this trip, we have to—" Spencer peers over his shoulder toward the *Queen Anne's Revenge*.

"Yep, we have to be on the platform at the top of the main mast," Ethan finishes.

Spencer peers into the distance and his forehead wrinkles. "The physics would work," he mumbles. "Given the available data, we could posit—"

"Somebody stab me with a cutlass," Jake moans, "before Professor Spencer's explanation bores me to death."

Ethan fishes an old-fashioned pocket watch from his jeans, a timepiece inherited from his grandfather. On the first trip though time, the boys discovered that time travel jumbles electronic equipment. Palm pads, digital watches, and high-tech tablets are useless in the past. But an antique watch filled with gears and springs works fine.

"Does anybody know what time we arrived?" Ethan asks.

"Around 10:20 last night," Spencer says.

"So we should make it back to the ship just in time for the next hourly pulse," Ethan estimates.

"You want to catch the next bus?" Jake asks.

"My dad is definitely not on the ship. Besides, I've seen enough blood," Ethan sighs. "I'll never feel the same about pirates after this."

As they've been rowing, the weather has shifted. Black clouds hide the sun. By the time they are hoisted aboard *Queen Anne's Revenge,* a cold wind is whining through the rigging, and droplets of rain splatter the deck. As the cockboat is lashed down, Blackbeard meets them.

"We found water, but no fruit," Liz tells him.

"And Chappy?" the captain asks, studying Ethan with newfound respect.

"Chappy and the swabber settled

their differences," Liz answers, letting Blackbeard draw his own conclusion.

"If you're not needed on deck," Blackbeard grunts, eyeing the sky, "best seek your quarters until this blows over. It won't last long."

But the time travelers ignore the coming squall, and make their way to the main mast.

 TURN TO PAGE 172.

# KING OF THE SEVEN SEAS

Even on the stormiest sea, God is still in control. No matter how wet and wild this pirate adventure becomes, the Time Crashers know that God is in charge.

Below is a reverse-alphabet message from Psalm 89:9 about the true King of the sea. Maybe this psalm was written by someone who sailed on the ocean. To figure out the message, just change A to Z, and B to Y, and C to X, and so on. Reverse alphabet! Get it?

BLF IFOV LEVI GSV HFITRMT HVZ;
DSVM RGH DZEVH NLFMG FK, BLF HGROO GSVN.

See answers on page 200.

TIME CRASHERS

"We arrived in a storm," Spencer sighs. "We might as well leave the same way."

Ethan grabs the nearest ratline. "Last monkey to the top is a rotten banana!"

As they climb, the wind gusts fiercely and a light rain slicks the ropes. The rain grows heavier by the time they reach the first of the three platforms on the main mast. A bolt of lightning forks across the sky. They climb with care in the blinding rain. Their ears echo with the roar of thunder. Finally they scramble onto the highest platform and lock arms around the mast, their wet forms pressed together.

"Hey, look!" Jake cries.

Flickering fingers of light dance on the tip of the mast overhead. Purple electricity writhes in the stormy air.

"St. Elmo's fire," Spencer shouts. "A harmless effect of the ionized air from the storm. But extremely fascinating."

The boys feel their hair stand on end, and then the familiar tingle of the retrieval pulse worms through their bellies.

"Twenty-first century, here we come," Ethan says.

But he's wrong.

Instead of the wrenching passage through time that the boys have come to expect, they feel suddenly weightless. Darkness engulfs them. The storm vanishes.

An electric hiss sizzles in the black emptiness.

ZZZSSSTZZSSZTZZZZZ!

Suddenly they stand in a steamy jungle. A shadow passes over them, and Ethan looks up. A pterodactyl circles lazily overhead, wings outstretched like a leather kite. A rumbling snort jerks the time traveler's attention back to the earth. A Tyrannosaurus rex lifts his bloody head from a fresh kill. The boys stare with wide eyes, feet rooted to the ground and hearts frozen with icy terror. The monster turns his fearsome face slowly in their direction and sniffs the damp air. A tiny clawed hand drags a dangling piece of raw meat from the corner of its mouth. Black, heartless eyes fix on the boys. Rows of

endless teeth appear as the reptilian mouth opens.

"Is it grinning?" Spencer asks in a choked voice.

FFZSSSTZZSSZTZZZSSHH!

The boys are in a dim room without chair, bed, or table. The walls and floor are made of mortared stones, large and rough. The ceiling of hand-planed beams is so low that Jake stoops to protect his head. A bearded man wrapped in ragged blankets sleeps on moldy straw, a fold of the wool cover drawn over his head. His shivering arms are wrapped around his ribs to ward off the chill air. He mutters in his slumber, and shouts without waking. Thrashing in the grip of the nightmare, he turns his face into the single beam of pale moonlight slanting through a barred window. The blanket falls away and Ethan gasps.

VVSSSZZZSSSTZZSSZTFF!

The boys squint against blazing sunshine. They sniff dusty air and hard-packed earth. Their vision adjusts and they see an arena, its rough plank seats are filled with cheering men and women. The earth shudders, and they turn to find themselves in the path of a charging knight on horseback. The sun glints brilliantly on the knight's armor. His face hidden behind a visor, the warrior bears down on them. His galloping mount snorts fiercely; driving hooves hurl clods of brown dirt into the air. The knight kicks armored heels into the flanks of the horse, urging him to greater speed. He extends his lance. A red pennant flaps on the long shaft, and the deadly point is aimed at Ethan's heart, only inches from skewering the time traveler.

FFFSSTZZSSZTZZSHHTTT!

Desert sand swirls beneath the feet of the Time Crashers. A bearded man clutching a wooden staff lifts his hands toward the sky. Tumbling clouds boil in the heavens. The air is charged with tension, and they sense that something is about to happen. A crowd of frightened faces shrinks back from the commanding figure. Men murmur uneasily; some of the women weep.

"Now you will see the power of the Lord!" the bearded man thunders.

He stiffens his upraised arms, wiry muscles flexing. A sudden wind whips through the crowd. Clouds of billowing sand darken the sun, and stinging grains razor through the air.

SSHHHTZZSSZTZZZ! BOOM!

The boys are back on the platform, rain lashing them, their arms locked on the mast.

"Let's …" Ethan chokes. "Let's get down."

As they slither down the ratlines, Spencer's mind is at work. "The charge from the St. Elmo's fire disrupted the retrieval pulse," he pants. "We were bouncing through time."

"What a trip!" Jake says. "Better than the Screaming Death Whirl at the state fair."

When they safely reach the deck, Blackbeard is waiting. The rain plasters his long beard to his chest. His eyes are unreadable.

"Quite a show up there," he rumbles. "The St. Elmo's fire, and then you appearing and disappearing. Or so it seemed in the lightning. Half my men think it was a good omen. The rest fear you've brought bad luck on us."

He rocks back on his heels, thumbs hitched in his belt.

"Personally, I don't believe in such things," he says agreeably, "but I won't have my crew upset by superstition. So the next man who climbs that mast without my permission will catch a musket ball halfway to the top. I hope we have an understanding, lads."

The captain strides away undaunted by the wind and driving rain, as if he were fiercer than the storm.

Ethan stares into the wild weather, rain dripping unnoticed down his face.

"Hey, boss-man, you okay?" Jake asks.

Ethan turns haunted eyes toward his friends. "Did you see the man in the dungeon?"

"Sure," they both agree.

"The light was bad. The beard covered half his face. We were only there for a second or two, but …" Ethan swallows hard. "I think it was my dad."

"That means he's still alive!" Spencer cries.

"If he's out there somewhere," Jake says, slamming a fist into his palm, "we won't quit looking until we bring him home."

Ethan nods in silence. Not all the wetness running down his cheeks is from the rain.

 CONTINUE TO **PAGE 180**.

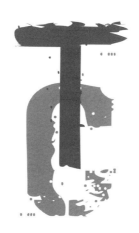

The storm blows over as quickly as it rose. Under clear skies and bright stars, *Queen Anne's Revenge* sails through the night while the exhausted Time Crashers sleep below decks—Spencer in a hammock, the other two on rag piles.

As on their first morning on the ship, it is Long Liz who greets them at sun up. Catching the edge of Spencer's hammock, she rolls him onto the floor.

Rubbing his head, Spencer asks her, "Do you take annoying pills, or are you always like this?"

"Rumors are buzzing like fruit flies, lads," Liz says in a conspiratorial voice. "King George is offering amnesty to any pirate who will promise to cease his looting."

"Amnesty?" Jake asks.

"All crimes cancelled," Spencer says. "Any pirate who chooses amnesty is a free man with no charges against him."

"Sweet deal," Jake says. "Will Blackbeard take it?"

"Some say yes," Liz tells them, "and some say no."

"What do you say?" Spencer asks.

"I say we're sailing into Topsail Inlet to careen the ships," Liz tells them, "so you softies are about to get a taste of real work. Although it won't be any tougher than climbing the mainmast in a lightning storm. What were you thinking yesterday? Why is the top of that mast so important to you?"

The pirate lass studies them shrewdly for a moment before departing. After Liz leaves, Ethan explains that careening the ships means dragging them ashore so the hulls can be scraped clean of barnacles and the cracks caulked with tar.

"I gotta see this," Jake says eagerly, heading up the ladder to the deck.

Ethan grabs his arm and pulls him back. "There's more," Ethan whispers. "You're about to see Blackbeard at his tricky worst."

Eyes wide, Jake settles beside Spencer on the damp floor. Ethan looks around to be sure they're alone.

"Blackbeard is going to run the *Queen Anne's Revenge* aground, supposedly by accident. Then he'll tie lines to another ship and Israel Hands will pretend he's trying to free *Queen Anne's Revenge* from the sand bar. But what he'll really be doing is grounding the rescue ship as well. When both ships are sinking, Blackbeard and Hands will board

the ship *Adventure.* They'll leave the other ships and pirates to take care of themselves, while Blackbeard and his favorites sail away on the *Adventure* with all the treasure and loot."

"So Blackbeard gets amnesty from his crimes and piles of money for a cushy retirement," Jake says. "A pile he splits with one crew instead of six. You almost have to admire Cap'n Black Snake."

"What are we going to do about it?" Spencer asks.

"Nothing," Ethan decides. "It's thieves stealing from other thieves. Our job is to watch for a chance to get up that mast and catch the retrieval pulse."

The boys emerge on deck to a beautiful day. The rest of Blackbeard's ships have gathered at Topsail Inlet, the full fleet of six ships and 300 pirates.

In the next hours, everything happens just as Ethan predicted.

The pirate leader runs *Queen Anne's Revenge* aground on a nearby sand bar and soon entangles another ship in a fake rescue attempt. While attention is focused on the sinking ships, Captain Blackbeard, Israel Hands, and Long Liz slip into a dinghy and row unnoticed to the *Adventure*. At least, they are almost unnoticed. As the rowboat pulls away, Ethan waves his red ball cap to Liz and she lifts her tri-corner hat in reply.

"She told me she could take care of herself," Ethan says ruefully. "I guess she's right."

The other pirates, the ones left behind, begin to understand the situation. A storm of shouts and curses rings through the inlet.

"This will get ugly," Spencer predicts. "Maybe we should get out of sight."

 IF YOU THINK THE BOYS SHOULD HIDE IN THE NEARBY WOODS, CONTINUE TO **PAGE 185**.

 IF YOU THINK THE BOYS SHOULD STAY NEAR THE QUEEN ANNE'S REVENGE, TURN TO **PAGE 191**.

The boys steal away to a copse of trees not far from shore, and hide behind the trunks while the angry pirates rant, holler, and pass around bottles of rum. The boys settle into a low spot well-cushioned with fallen leaves.

"So Blackbeard gets away with everything," Jake says in disgust.

"Not really," Ethan says. "A man like Blackbeard never knows when to quit. Oh, he gets a full pardon from Governor Eden. He buys a house and becomes respectable. For a while, Blackbeard is up to his hairy neck in North Carolina high society. He hangs with bankers and mayors, attends all the best parties, and flirts with the ladies."

Ethan settles into the dry leaves and folds his arms behind his head.

"But the peaceful life isn't enough for Blackbeard," Ethan continues. "He goes back to pirating. He keeps it secret for a while, but before long

185

everybody knows Blackbeard has returned to his old, ugly ways. It ends like this."

Ethan brushes a leaf from his cheek and drops his voice low. "Blackbeard attacks a ship called the *Jane*. The Commander, Richard

Maynard, hides his troops below deck until the raiders board. The pirates are surprised and suddenly outnumbered. Blackbeard fights to the end. He swings his sword so hard that it breaks Maynard's blade. But Blackbeard is surrounded. Someone hits him from behind, and

he finally goes down. By the time the battle is over, Blackbeard's body contains five gunshot wounds and more than twenty stabs from swords and knives."

"What about Blackbeard's crew?" Jake asks.

"Executed for piracy in Williamsburg, Virginia," Ethan answers. With a shudder, he adds, "Their dead bodies are hung in iron cages along the main road into town and left to rot as a warning to other pirates."

"All of them?" Spencer asks.

"Israel Hands was never captured," Ethan explains. "A few days before the attack on the *Jane*, Blackbeard shot his first mate in the knee during a card game. Hands had been put ashore to recover and he wasn't on board when they attacked the *Jane.* Some people say Blackbeard knew the end was near, and he didn't want his old friend Hands to go down with him."

"And Long Liz?" Jake asks uneasily.

"There's no Liz Miller on the list of captured pirates," Ethan assures him. "I hope Liz took her loot and bought a farm, but we'll never know."

After a few hours of anger and three drunken sword fights that end without injuries, the abandoned crewmen climb onto the remaining ships. Some loudly declare that they should overtake Blackbeard and reclaim their share of the loot. Others argue with equal volume that they should strike out on their own and elect a new captain. The arguments continue as the ships sail around a bend in the Carolina coast and disappear from view.

When the boys emerge from their hiding place in the woods, their hearts hammer in panic. The shifting tide has pulled the *Queen Anne's Revenge* off the sand bar, and the foundering ship is sinking beneath the blue waters. Part of the bow is still above water, as are the topmost lengths of the fore mast and main mast. The weight of the heavy cannons speeds the sinking. With each passing minute, more of the doomed vessel slides beneath the sea.

As they run to the water's edge, Ethan checks his watch. Twenty minutes before the next pulse. Can the *Queen Anne's Revenge* remain afloat that long?

"Nice day for a swim," Jake says, cleaving the water in a perfect dive.

Ethan and Spencer follow, and all three stroke to the mainmast. The

two lower platforms are already under water. Inch by inch and minute by minute, more of the mast slips beneath the surface. The boys hang onto the mast, waiting helplessly for the retrieval pulse to activate. Time crawls as slowly as the hours in a school day. The platform that promises their route home is completely submerged. With an abrupt plunge and a groan, the rest of the ship sinks beneath the rising tide.

"Follow that ship," Jake shouts.

"Take a dozen quick, shallow breaths," Spencer advises, "and then fill your lungs. That's how the pearl divers do it."

The water is clear enough that the boys locate the mast and the platform with ease, but the pressure pounds their eardrums and tries to squeeze the air from their chests. As Ethan clings to the waterlogged

wood, he struggles to keep calm.

*Any minute now,* he tells himself. *The pulse is on the way.*

His lungs burn and he wants a breath of air more than anything else in the world. Tiny stars swim before his eyes. His senses spin dizzily.

He wonders, *Is that the tingle of the retrieval pulse or is this how it feels to drown?*

*Don't let go of that platform,* he orders his hand. *No matter what I decide to do, you hang on, fingers.*

Blackness fills his head.

His lungs ache. Air bubbles from his mouth and nose.

His fingers weaken.

*This is …*

Suddenly he vanishes from the year 1718, and the ocean swirls into the space left by his disappearing body.

## THE END

TURN TO THE EPILOGUE ON PAGE 195.

W e haven't done anything wrong," Ethan insists. "Why would they be angry with us?"

"We're about to find out," Spencer says.

A knot of enraged pirates notices the boys and stalks toward them.

"You lubbers have brought us nothing but bad luck," says a lanky pirate with a droopy eye.

The other pirates murmur agreement.

"But we know how to get rid of bad luck," Droopy says. "Don't we boys?"

"We throw it in the sea," declares a pirate with a puckered scar on his cheek.

"That's right," Droopy agrees.

"But first we make sure it doesn't float," Scar adds, flashing a cutlass.

The pirates surround the boys in a ring of drawn blades.

"Blackbeard's your enemy," Ethan says reasonably. "How will it help you to cut us down?"

"It might make us feel better," Droopy says. He laughs heartily.

"Let's find out," Scar says, advancing on Ethan with sword in hand.

A deep-throated boom rolls over the waves from the direction of the departing *Adventure*. A whistle slices the air.

Droopy shouts, "Cannon!" and dives for the sand.

An instant later, a cannon ball smashes the mainmast on the grounded *Queen Anne's Revenge*. The top of the great spar and the spying platform rip free and pinwheel through the air, thudding onto the nearby shore. The huddled pirates cower from the flying splinters.

"Take cover!" Scar shouts, and they scatter inland.

The other pirates on the beach follow them into the trees and brush.

In minutes, only Ethan, Jake, and Spencer stand on the shore. On the receding *Adventure*, Long Liz balances on the rail and makes a mock curtsy.

The boys wave back.

"Some people know how to make an entrance," Ethan says. "Liz knows how to make an exit."

"Speaking of exits," Jake says, standing beside the top platform on the fallen mast, "the bus is on the way."

The other boys join him, and an electric tingle races along their spines.

"That was quite a shot," Jake says, "at least if she was aiming for the mast."

"Do you think she was trying to put the top of the mast in reach for us?" Spencer wonders.

"Nah, she just wanted to scatter the pirates," Jake insists.

Ethan lifts his ball cap and wipes sweat from his forehead. "She must have overheard some of our conversations. But surely she didn't figure out that we're time travelers."

The boys look at each other uncertainly. They glance back at Long Liz, who is still watching them, as if waiting for something.

A moment later, the retrieval pulse carries them back to the 21st century. Long Liz Miller stares long and hard at the spot where the boys just vanished. She tips her head toward the empty beach and smiles a secret smile.

"I wish he'd left that hat," she mutters.

## THE END

TURN TO THE EPILOGUE ON PAGE 195.

# Epilogue

The boys materialize in the red glow of the basement laboratory. Thankfulness floods Ethan's heart as his gaze sweeps the familiar room.

"I can hardly believe we're back in our own time," Spencer says. He kneels and lovingly lays his palm on the concrete. "Feel that floor? It's not moving! There's no ocean rocking under us. I never thought I'd be so happy to stand still."

"What a wild ride," Ethan says.

Spencer nods. "I think this trip has changed us. At least, I feel different. The next time we're in a tough spot, I'm not going to give up hope. Just because I can't think of a way out, doesn't mean God can't make a way. God knows more than I do."

"Yeah," Jake agrees, "but he's probably the only one who does."

"I feel different, too," Ethan admits, as he leads the way from the lab and locks the door behind them. "All along I've wanted to get my father back safe and sound. Somehow, I want it even more now. I'm ready to do whatever it takes, face any risk, make any sacrifice. I'm convinced my dad is alive and waiting for me. I'm afraid he might be in a bad place, and we are the only ones who can rescue him."

The boys climb the basement steps and emerge in the kitchen. The back door leads them to a sunny day, the warm light brightening the trees and grass.

"You're ready to go the second mile," Spencer says.

"Coach calls it giving 110%," Jake adds. He holds up his thumb and forefinger only half an inch apart. "This is the difference between winning and losing. Winners try this much harder and hold on this

much longer. That's all it takes, Ethan."

"I'll hang on as long as it takes to bring Dad home," Ethan says.

"The trip has changed me, too," Jake says, scuffing uneasily at the lawn with the toe of his running shoe. "Watching those pirates in action has made me feel so guilty."

Spencer and Ethan exchange concerned looks.

"Go ahead, big guy," Spencer encourages. "You can trust us."

"This is hard to admit to my best friends," Jake says, staring at the ground, "but—sometimes—I steal stuff."

"You're joking!" Ethan protests. "You wouldn't do that."

"But I do," Jake says, voice shaky. He looks up at his friends, his somber face suddenly breaking into a wide grin. "Every chance I get on the softball field, I steal bases."

Spencer grabs Jake's legs in a low tackle, and Ethan hits him high. Shouting and laughing, the three friends tumble into the warm grass.

In the hidden lab beneath Ethan's basement, the power crystal on the time machine glows a dull red, charging for the next trip into the past.

## THE END

# The Real Deal

During the Golden Age of Piracy, from the mid 1600s to the early 1700s, pirates of every description sailed the seas. Some were well-educated and cultured; others were coarse and brutal. Some turned to piracy in desperation, while others enjoyed the adventure and risk. A few pirates were extremely successful. Henry Avery, for instance, is estimated to have captured jewels and gold equal to almost one hundred million dollars in modern money. But most pirates never scored big hauls. Instead, they eked out a miserable living stealing bags of sugar and bales of tobacco—all the while eating rotten food and battling disease.

Edward Teach, better known as Blackbeard, is one of the most notorious pirates of all time. He was active as a pirate for only a couple of years, but Blackbeard's legend lives-on in books and movies. His plundering days were spent in the West Indies and along the eastern coast of the American colonies. (Remember, America wouldn't become an independent nation for another sixty years after the pirate's death.) So many things about Blackbeard loom larger than life: his courage, his trickery, and that wild beard plaited with ribbons and stuffed with burning cannon wicks.

The Time Crashers meet Blackbeard shortly after one of his most daring adventures. In May 1718, Blackbeard's fleet anchored outside the port of Charleston, South Carolina. For more than a week they stopped—and demanded money from—every ship that came or went from Charleston. Blackbeard even captured some important citizens and held them for ransom until medical supplies were delivered to his crew.

Blackbeard finally met the same end as many pirates—a violent death—but piracy lives on in the modern world. In some places, pirates still attack, steal, and kidnap people from helpless ships. Nowadays, pirates use speedboats, automatic firearms, and explosives to spread fear and destruction. The methods change, but the goal is still the same: stealing and killing.

Even though he enjoyed their adventures in books, Ethan was disappointed to meet pirates in real life. As Jake discovered, "These are not nice people."

## WOULD YOU WANT TO MEET A PIRATE?

## THE TEN ARTICLES - PAGE 24

worship, fake gods, misuse, holy day, father and mother, kill, marriage vows, steal, tell lies, wishing for things

## DEAD END? - PAGE 46

All that night the LORD drove the sea back with a strong east wind and turned it into dry land. The waters were divided, and the Israelites went through the sea on dry ground. (Exodus 14:21-22)

## OUR PROTECTOR - PAGE 60

The LORD is my strength and my shield! (Psalm 28:7)

## WAR AND PEACE - PAGE 105

Wisdom is better than weapons of war. (Ecclesiastes 9:18)

## TREASURE HUNTING - PAGE 139

You will seek me and find me when you seek me with all your heart. (Jeremiah 29:13)

## DOLLARS AND SENSE - PAGE 164

Keep your lives free from the love of money and be content with what you have. (Hebrews 13:5)

## KING OF THE SEVEN SEAS - PAGE 171

You rule over the surging sea; when its waves mount up, you still them. (Psalm 89:9)